THE QUEEN OF OCEAN PARKWAY

SARVENAZ
TASH

ALFRED A. KNOPF  NEW YORK

THIS IS A BORZOI BOOK PUBLISHED BY ALFRED A. KNOPF

Visit us on the Web! rhcbooks.com

Educators and librarians, for a variety of teaching tools, visit us at RHTeachersLibrarians.com

Library of Congress Cataloging-in-Publication Data
Names: Tash, Sarvenaz, author.
Title: The queen of Ocean Parkway / Sarvenaz Tash.
Description: First edition. | New York : Alfred A. Knopf, 2024. | Audience: Ages 8–12.
Summary: Eleven-year-old podcaster-turned-sleuth, Roya,
teams up with the new kid in the building, Amin, to find their missing neighbor.
Identifiers: LCCN 2024003976 (print) | LCCN 2024003977 (ebook)
ISBN 978-0-593-80978-5 (hardcover) | ISBN 978-0-593-80979-2 (library binding)
ISBN 978-0-593-80980-8 (ebook) | Subjects: CYAC: Missing persons—Fiction.
Apartment houses—Fiction. | Blessing and cursing—Fiction. | New York (N.Y.)—Fiction.
Mystery and detective stories. | LCGFT: Detective and mystery fiction. | Novels.
Classification: LCC PZ7.T2111324 Qu 2024 (print) | LCC PZ7.T2111324 (ebook) | DDC [Fic]—dc23

The text of this book is set in 9.5-point Sienna.

Editors: Erin Clarke and Katherine Harrison | Designer: Carol Ly
Production Editor: Melinda Ackell | Managing Editor: Jake Eldred
Production Manager: Natalia Dextre

Printed in the United States of America
10 9 8 7 6 5 4 3 2 1
First Edition

TO THE REAL BENNETT
AND JONAH, MY KOOPS.
OUR BROOKLYN ADVENTURES
ARE MY FAVORITE.

AND TO MY
GRANDMOTHERS,
AGHDAS AND MOAZAZ, WHO I THINK
GUIDED THIS ONE FROM WHEREVER
THEY ARE. I LOVE YOU, I MISS YOU,
I'M SO GRATEFUL FOR ALL MY
BEAUTIFUL MEMORIES OF YOU.

Petrov Family

IVAN

NATASHA

POLINA

ANNIKA

SOFIA

DARIA

INESSA

STEFANIE

KATYA

TORI

The Accidental Spy

ROYA CALLED THE BOYS FROM 6D Bumblebee and Bear for the podcast—though those were not their real names, of course. She watched them leave the apartment building, living up to their code names as Bumblebee flitted about in bursts of energy while Bear cuddled close to his dad.

They were on their way to summer camp, and Roya didn't like the little garden snake that was twisting its way around her stomach. She knew what it was: jealousy. That they had someplace to go, someplace that—from everything she had heard and read—sounded like it was filled with archery and electric scooters and swimming around in a gigantic pool right at the edge of the Verrazzano Bridge. She was even jealous that they had each other to chatter to: siblings seemed like built-in friends.

But this wouldn't do at all. Jealousy was a feeling that Roya couldn't find a solution for. And Roya was a girl who liked solutions, a problem-solver. That's why she was so good at her job.

Okay, fine, that's why Aty, her mom, was so good at *her* job. As the super of their large Brooklyn apartment building, Aty was in charge of seventy-two apartments and over 250 tenants. But even if Roya wasn't technically on the payroll, she knew she was a large part of her mom's success. After all, how else would Aty have known that Mrs. Bernstein in 4E needed an ambulance called because she hadn't gone to visit Mrs. Kowalska in 3E for a whole day and a half? Or that *some*one (namely, two-year-old Josh in 1K, known to Roya's listeners as Kleptosaurus) was stealing all the plastic T. rexes that were in the community playroom?

And then there was Roya's other job: her secret one, the one she turned to now in her most desperate time of need—otherwise known as the bottomless boredom of a summer vacation spent alone in her apartment. Roya Alborzi: podcast host.

"What *can* be the cause of the Great Bathtub Clog of 5J?" Roya spoke in a low voice into her pocket recorder. "A Guinness World Record–setting hairball? A naked mole rat? A portal into another dimension? Whatever it is, this reporter is determined to get to the bottom of it." She had moved to the storage room in the basement, the one she'd discovered had the best acoustics for recording. The voice recorder had been a gift from her parents for her eleventh birthday, at her dad's suggestion since he and Roya listened to all those science podcasts together. Though neither Aty nor Baba had been privy to anything she had made on it—for obvious reasons.

Roya waited to turn the recorder off before letting out a sigh, tapping her pen on the open page of her journal. She didn't have a full script yet. And to be honest, she wasn't feeling too confident that this was going to turn into the riveting episode she was striving for.

She flipped through her notes just to see if there was another apartment or tenant that might make for a better episode. The red leather-bound journal was supposed to be her "feelings journal," which was code for "anger journal"—and why, Roya suspected, Aty had chosen the red color. But Roya had quickly found that a better way to control her feelings, including anger, was not to write about them, but to write about other people. Particularly the other people in her building.

And Roya did consider it *her* building. Even though it had been built over a hundred years before she was born, she doubted anyone knew more about the regal bricks, the rickety, old-fashioned elevators, or even the hidden graffiti on the bottom of the stairs between floors three and four. Her parents had moved here when Aty was five months pregnant with Roya, so every single one of her memories was tied to this grand, old building with the weeping willow in the front. Roya once heard an older resident call the building the Queen of Ocean Parkway, and that's exactly how she'd thought of it ever since. She'd even named her podcast after it.

And this Queen was *alive.* Sure, she was old, and there wasn't a first-time delivery person who didn't get confused by having to manually pull open the door of the ancient elevator, but this Queen had seen more things—more lives, more stories, more wars, more pandemics, more births, and more deaths—than any one person in existence.

Roya dedicated the journal to her, and it now did double duty as her manual for both of her jobs. She used the journal to document ordinary things like when the elevator broke down (at least once every other week) and when the boiler needed fixing—things she'd need to report to her mom. But she also wrote about the residents, facts and observations and speculations that often found their way into her podcast. Each episode was dedicated to one apartment and the residents who lived in it, though for their privacy, and hers, she changed their names. Even the Queen went by her initials—the podcast was titled *QOOP* on all platforms. In her heart of hearts, Roya suspected that she was born to be an investigative journalist: someone who found out the truth about things. Though, right now, she settled for honing her storytelling skills—like when she took a deep dive into why exactly the family in 4J (the Wacky Thwackers) could sometimes be heard hammering deep into the night: Were they experimental percussionists deeply invested in their craft, or were they practicing for a prison break?

But nothing seemed to be holding Roya's interest for long today. She left the storage room, thinking maybe she'd try again after a snack. She was lost in her thoughts when the elevator door opened, revealing two people.

"Good morning, Roya." It was Katya and Stefanie from 3G. Katya had a basket of laundry in her arms, and Stefanie was in her maroon hospital scrubs.

"Good morning," Roya said enthusiastically. Katya and Stefanie were two of her very favorite tenants. They were in their late twenties, and when they'd gotten married two years ago, Roya and her parents had been guests. Stefanie was an ER resident too and usually had some interesting story to tell about who had walked into her hospital that week.

"Did you see that a new restaurant opened on Church Avenue?" Katya asked Roya. "I think it's called Taste of Bangla. Do you want to try it out with us next week?"

"I'd love to," Roya said.

"It's a date! Right, Stefanie?" Katya turned to Stefanie, and Roya was surprised to see that Stefanie didn't look enthusiastic at all. In fact, she was frowning.

"Right," she mumbled. The two of them had already started to walk away when Stefanie added to Katya, "In order for us to go on this date, you would still have to be here next week."

"Of course I'm going to be here," Katya said with a laugh. "Where else would I be?"

They had turned the corner and their voices were fading away when Roya heard Stefanie say, "I don't know! Where did all the rest of your family go? You know that fortune is cursed!"

Hold up, what? The elevator door closed, and Roya let it without getting on. Instead, she tiptoed a little farther down the hall and crouched behind one of the concrete pillars that hid her from view of the laundry room. Now she could hear better as Katya gave a snort. "Stefanie. You're a doctor. A curse? Really?"

"That's what your grandmother said too!" Stefanie replied. "And your great-grandmother. And your aunt." Roya peeked out from behind the pillar. A flush that matched Stefanie's scrubs had crept over her rich brown skin. "And you know where they all ended up, Katya?"

"No," Katya replied, her own pale skin remaining cool and unchanged, her blond bun still perfectly in place. She was calmly loading laundry into one of the machines.

"*Exactly!*" Stefanie's long indigo and black braids swished in irritation. "*Nobody* knows. They're gone. Grandmother is not a chance to change our fortunes. She's a curse."

"But she did change our family's fortunes," Katya said as she pushed the door of the washing machine closed and put in her quarters. Roya held her breath, desperate to hear more. "And I don't believe in curses. But I know we *need* that money." She pressed a button to start the machine's gentle cycle before she scooted her laundry basket close to the pillar, just a few inches from Roya's nose, and turned on her ballet flats. From her low vantage point, Roya could see how worn down the soles were.

"What good is money if you're gone, Katya?" Stefanie pleaded. They were heading back to the elevator, and Roya had to employ some ninja-like tactics to move herself around to the other side of the pillar without being noticed. Just in time too.

"I won't disappear. I've taken precautions," Katya said as they headed down the hallway, their voices fading.

"Precautions? What possible precautions could guarantee you'd be safe?"

"Twenty-first-century precautions that the rest of my family never had access to. Trust me. I'll be fine. Besides, I'm not even technically my aunt's 'daughter,' like the fortune said. Probably nothing will happen at all."

The elevator door slid shut on their conversation.

But Roya had heard enough: A fortune? A curse? She *had* to get to the bottom of this. It was perfect podcast material. She would start by snagging an interview with Katya and Stefanie.

Except that twenty-four hours later, Katya was gone.

2
A Familiar Stranger

AS SOON AS SHE GOT back to her apartment that morning, Roya wrote down the date and time that she'd seen Katya and Stefanie in the laundry room, that they'd thrown around the words *curse* and *fortune,* and mentioned something about Katya's relatives disappearing. She was thinking about recording an intro when 5J's bathtub overflowed again and Aty called Roya and an army of old towels to active duty.

But that night, when Roya went to put the dirty towels into one of the washing machines, she was surprised to find that Katya's clothes had been left in a brown laundry basket on one of the tables. The residents would occasionally unload someone else's laundry when they needed a machine. Sometimes clothes could even be left for a few hours, but this was now closing in on almost twelve hours later.

Roya inspected the clothes briefly—they seemed pretty

standard: T-shirts and underwear and socks. She made a note in her journal about them being left there. It felt mysterious, so maybe she could use it as a cliff-hanger for a segment of her podcast. She went to sleep thinking about how she might work it in.

The next morning, Aty sent her out to the corner hardware store to get a new drain snake for the bathtub in 5J. Which was why Roya saw the two police officers leave the building but missed the entire conversation they had with her mom.

"What happened?" Roya asked Aty. "Was it about Katya?"

"Yes," Aty said as she took the drain snake from her. "How would you know that?"

"Because I overheard Katya and Stefanie having a strange conversation yesterday. And then they didn't pick up her laundry last night," Roya replied.

"Overheard?" Aty squinted her eyes in that X-ray vision way she sometimes had with her daughter.

"Yup," Roya said. She didn't really need to go into details about her little spy experiment.

"I see," Aty said. "Why don't you go try to catch the officers outside and tell them."

Roya raced out the door, past the small courtyard, and down the few stairs at the front of the Queen, but she didn't see anyone. The cop car that had been illegally parked at her corner was no longer there.

She walked back into the building dejectedly. "They're gone," she said as the door shut behind her, but she was speaking to an empty lobby. Aty was gone too.

"For what it's worth, I don't think they would have listened anyway," came a small voice.

Okay, so the lobby wasn't empty. A boy about Roya's age sat on the bottom stair across from her apartment. He was dressed in khaki shorts and a black T-shirt with the letter F in an orange circle printed on it. He must belong to the family that had moved into the building only a couple of weeks ago. Roya had helped Aty put up *Welcome Home* balloons in the lobby the week they'd moved in, but the family had, up until now, kept to themselves. Which was why Roya didn't know the boy. Yet.

"Hi," she said as she walked over. "I'm Roya. I'm the super's kid." She pointed toward 1A, where the word *SUPER* was stuck on with mailbox letters she and Aty had picked up from the hardware store a few years ago.

"Amin," the boy said. "We just moved into—"

"2A," Roya replied. "I know. So did you hear what the cops asked?"

Amin nodded. He had a large mass of jet-black hair so shiny, it could have come from one of the creepy porcelain dolls that Mrs. Sweetin in 1H was always trying to get Roya to show interest in. "Officer Park said"—Amin cleared his throat and put on a slightly deeper voice—"'I don't want you to worry. We just got a call from a Ms. Turner in apartment 3G. Her wife, an Ekaterina . . .' And here, the officer checked his notes before continuing, 'An Ekaterina Petrov apparently left yesterday and hasn't returned.'

"And then his partner, Officer Robbins, said"—Amin pitched his voice a little higher—"'In most cases, they turn back up. Most likely she and Ms. Turner had a fight, and Ms. Petrov went somewhere to cool off. But we figured we'd ask if you know anything about them as a couple, whether they fought a lot or anything like that. We'll take a statement.'"

Roya watched Amin, slightly in awe. "Is this a word-for-word reenactment of their conversation?"

Amin shrugged. "I have an echoic memory. It's kinda like a photographic memory, but for sounds."

"Wow," Roya said. "That's amazing."

"Some people call it annoying?"

"Who?" Roya asked.

"Uh . . . sometimes my dad. Like when my mom tells him she told him to do something and he says she didn't, and then she turns to me to prove that yes, she did." He gave a shy smile.

"Like a human recorder. Wow." Roya returned his smile. "I write down things that happen in my journal, but otherwise I wouldn't be able to remember anything so well. Anyway, go on. What happened next?"

Feeding off Roya's enthusiasm, Amin jumped up and proceeded to reenact the rest of the conversation, leaping from one side of the staircase to the other when he was playing Officer Park, Officer Robbins, or Aty—whose Persian accent he had down pat too. It was like watching a one-man play.

ATY: Katya has lived in this building all her life. In fact, her great-great-grandparents moved here right around when the building was built.

OFFICER PARK: Hmph. I'd be dying to know how much they pay in rent, then.

ATY: It's rent-controlled. So, yes, they pay much less than most apartments in this neighborhood. Anyway, I've known Stefanie since she moved in five years ago, and she's just lovely. No history of violence or anything you're talking about. They're a very nice couple.

OFFICER PARK: Okay, then. Like we said, nine times out of ten, she'll turn up here within a few hours, and that'll be the end of that.

OFFICER ROBBINS: Thank you for your time, Ms. Alborzi.

"Then my mom corrected him about her last name," Roya guessed. "'It's Zonouzi,'" she said, trying her own hand at affecting Aty's voice.

Amin nodded. "How did you know?"

"It's a pet peeve with her. My parents are divorced, but she never changed her name, even when they were married. Though I know the buzzer still says 'The Alborzis.' Anyway, what happened next?"

"Officer Robbins told your mom to let them know when she sees Ms. Petrov. Then she gave your mom her card and left," Amin related.

"They said *when* she sees her, not *if?*" Roya asked.

"Yup," Amin said.

"Like they fully expect Katya to come waltzing through that front door any minute? Like she's away at a sleepover?" Roya snorted incredulously.

"I guess," Amin replied. "What was it you had to tell them?"

"I overheard a conversation in the laundry room. I don't have your gift, but . . ." Roya hesitated for a split second. She hadn't shared what was in her journal with *any*body, let alone a person she had met for the first time less than five minutes ago. Yet there was something about Amin that felt so oddly familiar—like not only had they met before but they knew each other well, almost as if they were friends. Good friends. "Hold on," she said, then took out her key and ran inside her apartment, going straight for the small green safe under her bed. She punched in the four-digit code and, when it sprang open, grabbed her notebook and ran back to the stairs.

"Okay," Roya said as she opened her journal. "Yesterday at 8:55 in the morning, Katya was doing a load of laundry, and she said she was going after some fortune or something to do with a lot of money. Stefanie told her the fortune was cursed and that was the reason why Katya's great-grandmother, grandmother, and aunt had all disappeared. Katya said she didn't believe in curses and that she'd taken precautions. Then they left. And Katya never came back for the laundry. It's still down there." Roya looked up at Amin, expecting a reaction to her dramatic reveal. But he was just gazing serenely into the distance.

"Interesting. And strange."

"I know," Roya said. "I should get my mom's phone and call the cops, right?"

Amin shrugged. "You could. But they probably won't believe you. Take it from me: they never believe the person who knows the truth, not until it's too late."

Roya looked at Amin curiously, and a phrase that a few of the tenants used for her sprang to mind: *wise beyond your years.* But then again, when people said this, Roya thought it mostly meant they didn't expect much from kids. Which was *why* she knew so much in the first place: grown-ups tended to have lots of conversations in front of her thinking she wouldn't understand. Now here was Amin, a kid who not only understood the conversations, but memorized them word for word. A useful ally. "Do you know where my mom went?" she asked him.

"She didn't say," Amin started, but then Roya realized she could guess this answer on her own.

"I bet she went to talk to Stefanie," she said, brushing past Amin and pounding up the stairs. They'd be much faster than the hundred-year-old elevator. She stopped on the second landing and looked down at Amin. "You coming?"

For a moment, Amin looked shocked to be asked, and then his face broke out in a huge grin. "Yeah!" he said, and thundered up right behind Roya.

The Tearful Doctor

ROYA WAS RIGHT, OF COURSE, and they found Aty at the door of 3G, one arm around a teary-eyed Stefanie. The doctor was dressed in her dark maroon scrubs again—or maybe she had never changed out of them the day before—and the whites of her eyes nearly matched her outfit. Stefanie leaned against the door because it looked like if she didn't have a wall to support her, she wouldn't be able to stand.

"The officers assured me they'd find her," Aty was saying to her soothingly. "They said nine times out of ten, a missing person comes back before the end of the day."

Stefanie shook her head. "Then this is going to be the tenth time, Aty. They won't find her." She brushed a lingering tear away from her cheek.

"Is this because of the curse?" Roya blurted out from behind her mom. Stefanie's eyes widened in shock.

"Roya . . . ," Aty started, and Roya was sure she was going to give her some menial task to keep her away from the cloud of grief that hung over this apartment. She had done the same thing when Mr. Xiao in 2B had died suddenly a few months ago.

But then Stefanie spoke up. "How . . . how do you know about the curse?"

Roya had a split second to decide what to say, but she knew the stakes were higher than getting into trouble for eavesdropping. Besides, Katya and Stefanie's conversation had taken place in the laundry room, a *communal* spot. Roya hadn't been doing anything wrong—or, at least, not super wrong. She glanced at Amin, then dove in. "I overheard you. Yesterday in the laundry room."

"Oh," Stefanie said in a small voice. "I didn't realize you were still there."

"What's this about a curse?" Aty asked.

Stefanie gave a small, bitter laugh. "You wouldn't believe me if I told you."

"I would," Roya said.

Stefanie's deep brown eyes looked into Roya's. "I'm sure you would," she said softly.

Aty put her arm around her daughter, and Roya knew it was a subtle cue to lead her away. "We're sorry to bother you, Stefanie. Please let us know if there's anything we can do."

Roya gently took her mother's arm off her. "I want to help.

Please. Maybe if you tell us the story of the curse, it'll help you remember something. A clue."

"Roya," Aty said, more sharply.

"A clue?" Stefanie asked, her eyebrows knitting together.

Roya nodded. "I'm good at picking up on those." She lifted her red notebook, which she just realized she'd been clutching this whole time.

"Roya. This isn't a game," Aty said in the brick-hard voice she used only when she was about to absolutely forbid Roya from doing something, which didn't happen very often.

"All right," Stefanie said suddenly.

"What?" Aty turned to her.

"Maybe Roya's right," she told Aty. "Maybe telling someone will help me figure it out. I certainly couldn't tell the police everything."

Roya's eyes shone with excitement, though she tried to be respectful and not let the eager feeling make her face break out into a full grin.

"I thought I heard your voice, Aty," a panicked voice called from the stairwell. It was Mr. Schwartz from 5J. "Did you get the supplies for the tub? Now I can't seem to turn the water off at all!"

"Oh!" Aty said, remembering the drain snake she was still carrying limply at her side. "Yes. Wait, you can't turn the water off?"

"No, it's already overflowed to the floor," Mr. Schwartz said.

Aty looked at Stefanie apologetically. "I'm sorry. I'll be back as soon as I can."

Stefanie nodded in understanding as Aty rushed up the stairs after Mr. Schwartz.

"You can still tell *us*, though, Stefanie," Roya said, pulling the hand of the boy behind her, who had clammed up for the entirety of the conversation. "This is Amin. He just moved here and he has an echoic memory. It can only help."

"Hello, Amin," Stefanie said.

Amin shyly lifted a hand in greeting.

"Well, then." Stefanie stood up to her full height, looking a lot more like the confident doctor Roya was used to seeing. "Why don't you both come in?"

4
Fortunes and Misfortunes

ROYA HAD NEVER SEEN THE inside of apartment 3G before. Even though she knew the goings-on of the Queen very well, she wasn't actually often *inside* most apartments other than her own. When her mom went to do repairs or check on things, Roya was usually in school or otherwise not invited along. And Katya and her family were longtime residents, so her apartment had never even been renovated or repainted or prepared for a new tenant.

3G was unlike any apartment Roya *had* seen. It didn't have a modern, open-plan living space, but separate rooms that made up the kitchen, dining room, and living room. As Stefanie led them through, Roya peeked into the kitchen and saw a faded linoleum floor, warm yellow walls, and a large stove that looked like it'd come from the same era as the building's elevators.

They reached the small living room through a doorway. The walls here were papered in bright florals, and the couches were floral too, though the riotous orange blossoms and red roses had faded with time. Yet they looked inviting, like, Roya imagined, how furniture in your grandmother's house might look. Though Roya had never met her own grandparents, only her great-uncle Khosrow, who lived in a senior facility that she used to visit when her dad was still well enough to take her.

Roya sat down and was pleased to find that the couch was as comfortable and cozy as it looked. She let herself sink into the cushions, while Stefanie asked her and Amin if they wanted water or tea.

"I'm okay," Roya said, at the same time that Amin declared, "I don't like tea."

Stefanie nodded. "It's an acquired taste. Maybe you'll like it when you're older."

"Maybe," Amin said. "But probably not."

Stefanie smiled faintly. "You're right. Maybe not."

"So . . . ," Roya said, opening her notebook. "You said you were going to tell us the story? Of the fortune and the curse?"

Stefanie sighed as she looked out her window onto Ocean Parkway, where a steady stream of traffic snaked by as always. She closed her eyes for a second, as if to let the soothing rumble of cars and trucks help her put her thoughts in order. She took a deep breath before opening her eyes again, and turned to Roya. "As I think you know, Katya's family has been here for a long time." Roya nodded, and Stefanie turned to Amin to further explain, "Almost a hundred years."

Amin's eyes got wide. "A hundred years? In this building?"

"In this very apartment," Stefanie said. "Some of the furniture is even Katya's great-great-grandmother's. And a lot of the fixtures are from back then too."

"Like the stove," Roya said.

"Yes, exactly. Your mom has told us a few times we can change it, but Katya . . ." Stefanie got a faraway look in her eye. "Her family is very important to her. And so is her family history. And if it's important to her, it's important to me. But . . ." Stefanie's voice hitched, and she chewed on her lip for a moment before continuing. "I assume you've been to Coney Island."

"Yes," Roya and Amin said at the same time.

And then Amin added, "Did you know this street was named Ocean Parkway because it was built to lead from Prospect Park to the Atlantic Ocean? At Coney Island?"

"I didn't know that," Roya said. "But that makes sense."

"Yeah, it was built in the 1870s and designed to look like the tree-lined streets of Paris. It was the country's first street to have a bike lane," Amin said.

Roya blinked at him. "Wow. You know a lot about Ocean Parkway, especially considering you've only lived here two weeks."

"Oh," Amin said. "Yeah. I, um, like history. Especially New York City history. My dad calls me a buff. It means I know a lot of little random things."

"Then you might be the perfect person to tell this to," Stefanie said. "Because this story has a lot to do with New York history. Particularly Brooklyn history."

"Really?" Amin asked, eyes wide.

Stefanie nodded. "The story goes like this. A hundred years ago, Katya's great-great-grandmother, Natasha, was a young woman. She had come from Russia just a few years before. She was part of a circus family. They were called the Traveling Petrovs, and they had toured Europe for decades. They were famous there—so much so that Natasha's husband, Ivan, took her last name, Petrov, when they married."

As Stefanie spoke, Roya started jotting down keywords and phrases in her notebook that would help her recall the details later: Great-Great-Grandmother Natasha. Circus Family: The Traveling Petrovs.

"When Natasha and Ivan came to America, they tried to get their acrobatic routine in with some of the bigger circuses here," Stefanie continued. "They were able to get a few gigs. But then Natasha had to stop performing because she got pregnant and then had a baby. Polina.

"One summer day, Ivan took Natasha and Polina to Coney

Island. He had just lost his latest job and told her it was a little getaway, to help them forget their troubles. But in reality, he wanted to show Natasha a surprise he'd been working on for her. He'd been picking up odd jobs over the past few years and had a hand in building some of the attractions at Coney Island, including the Wonder Wheel."

"The Wonder Wheel?!" Amin asked breathlessly. "That's so iconic."

"And fun," Roya added, thinking of all the times she'd ridden it with her parents—more often her dad. "Katya's great-great-grandfather helped build that?"

Stefanie nodded. "He did. But he also helped build something else. Natasha recognized it as soon as she saw it: it was a tall cabinet made of glass and wood with a wax figure inside. And that wax figure looked exactly like Natasha's beloved grandmother back home in Russia, right down to the tarot cards she was holding. Sure enough, the cabinet said, in big black letters, 'Grandmother's Predictions.'"

"Oh!" Amin said. "I remember that machine too."

"I'm not sure I do," Roya admitted.

"I'm not too surprised. It's easy to miss if you're not looking for it," Stefanie said. "But Natasha was enchanted by it. Ivan told her about how he and his friend, a mechanic named Cornelius Lank, had built the arcade machine. Ivan had modeled the wax figure off a picture of Natasha's grandmother, while Cornelius had worked out the mechanisms. If you put in ten cents, Grandmother would give you a prediction for your future."

"Cool!" Roya said.

"That's what Natasha thought too," Stefanie agreed. "When Ivan presented her with a dime, she eagerly put it in. And a little lavender piece of paper came out. In fact, we still have it." Stefanie walked over to a small, shiny black box that sat on their bookshelf and picked it up. On the top of the box was a hand-painted image of a girl in an orange-and-red leotard, riding a unicycle across a tightrope. Letters were painted all around the edges of the box, reading *The Marvelous Traveling Petrovs* in a fancy font. Stefanie carefully opened the box, removed a small, pale purple card from it, and handed it to Roya.

"'Invest every dime in radio,'" Roya read out loud.

"Turn it over," Stefanie said.

Roya read the other side, which said, in tiny writing, *Send your daughter back in 25 years*, along with a series of dates:

July 25, 1949

July 22, 1974

July 26, 1999

July 22, 2024

Roya had no idea where this story was going, but it was only getting more and more interesting. "But what does this mean?"

"Nobody knew. And Ivan was taken aback by the fortune," Stefanie continued. "He thought he'd seen all the fortunes Cornelius had put in, and they weren't as specific as this. But he shrugged it off, joking, 'What dimes do we have to invest? We just invested our last dime in her.' Natasha, on the other hand, she couldn't help feeling that Grandmother was addressing *her* specifically. Even if Ivan insisted it was just a piece of paper that had randomly come out of a machine with hundreds of pieces of paper in it."

"And then?" Roya asked.

"Natasha convinced Ivan to take the machine's advice. When he got a new job, and saved up a little money, Natasha made him invest it in RCA, a new radio company. And eventually those dimes became . . . well, they became a lot more than dimes. They allowed the three of them to move out of her parents' home. Into this apartment."

"The fortune!" Roya said, turning the card reverentially in her hand. "That's the money Katya was talking about yesterday."

"Yes," Stefanie said.

"So what's the curse?" Roya asked.

Stefanie took in a deep breath as she tapped the other side of the card.

"'Send your daughter back in twenty-five years'?" Amin murmured.

"Exactly," Stefanie said. "Natasha never forgot that. She took her daughter, Polina, back to Coney Island on that exact date in 1949." She pointed to the first of the series of dates. "Only . . . Polina disappeared."

Roya gasped. Amin's already large eyes seemed to grow rounder.

"But the fortune part?" Stefanie continued. "That came true. Suddenly Natasha had money in her bank account, and she didn't know how it had gotten there. But her daughter was gone, never to return, and she was left to raise her granddaughter—Polina's daughter, Annika—on her own."

"Oh no," Roya said, feeling a surge of sadness for these people she hadn't known existed ten minutes ago. When she glanced over at the black box, she couldn't help but feel that the painted woman on the unicycle suddenly looked sad and lonely too.

"Annika was just a baby. She didn't remember her mother. But once she was old enough to hear the full story from Natasha, she felt this strong urge to go and find her. So twenty-five years later, on that second date, she also went back to Grandmother's Predictions. And . . . the same thing happened."

"Which part?" Roya asked breathlessly. "The fortune?"

Stefanie nodded grimly. "And the disappearance. The same thing happened to Annika's daughter Daria—Katya's aunt. The family was having a lot of financial problems and in danger of being evicted from this apartment. But still, after the previous disappearances, Annika's husband was not about to let either of his daughters near Grandmother. Sofia, Katya's mom, listened. But Daria, well, she wasn't so great at listening to anyone telling her what to do. Like Katya herself . . ." Stefanie's voice broke. She stopped and took deep breaths until she could talk calmly again. "We needed money so we could start trying to have a family of our own. But I *begged* Katya not to do it, not to go see Grandmother."

"I know," Roya said quietly. "I heard you."

Stefanie nodded. "I know I'm a doctor, a woman of science, and I *shouldn't* believe in curses. But that's a lot of people gone, a lot of coincidences. I thought I had convinced Katya that it wasn't worth it, but she waited until I was at work, and then she went to Coney Island. I think she thought since the fortune said 'send your daughter,' and she was technically Daria's niece, it wouldn't work anyway." A tear slid down Stefanie's cheek.

"And she hasn't come back," Roya said.

Stefanie shook her head.

"And what about your bank account?" Roya asked. "Have you looked at it?"

Stefanie closed her eyes in pain. "I've been too afraid," she whispered. "Because if I do and there's more money in there—then it becomes real. Then I know she's gone forever."

"Her grandmas and aunt never came back?" Amin asked.

Stefanie shook her head. "Never."

"Can you check?" Roya asked gently. "The bank account?"

A wild look flashed in Stefanie's eyes. Roya had seen that look once, when a raccoon had gotten trapped inside one of the storage rooms in the basement and Aty and Roya had opened the door on it. Right before the creature bolted, he gave them a look of utter panic. "No," Stefanie whispered.

Roya lightly touched Stefanie's arm. "It might be the only way to know for sure."

Stefanie closed her eyes again, but after a moment, she let out a huge breath and said, "You're right."

Slowly, she retrieved her phone from the side table. Roya and Amin waited in silence as they watched Stefanie work the screen and presumably log into her bank account.

Her gasp of terror told them all they needed to know.

5

Neighbors, Not Strangers

"WE NEED TO GO TO Coney Island," Roya said.

After Stefanie had seen that astronomical number in her joint account with Katya, it had taken several minutes for the shock to wear off. Now she just looked miserable. Roya felt uneasy, but taking action was the only thing to do.

"We can't," Stefanie said. "It's dangerous."

"No, it's not," Amin chimed in. "You said it was specific to Katya's family. And those dates on the card. But millions of people must have used this machine on other days, and nothing has happened to them."

Stefanie nodded reluctantly. "I suppose that's true."

"Did you tell the police any of this?" Roya asked.

Stefanie gave a bitter laugh. "No. Katya's mom had all sorts of horror stories of when her own mom and then sister disappeared. Her dad kept going to the police, trying to convince them to look into it, even telling them about Grandmother. All it did was eventually make them suspicious of him. It was a complete nightmare."

"Where's Katya's mom now?" Roya asked. "Can we talk to her?"

Stefanie shook her head. "She passed away from cancer five years ago."

At the word *cancer,* Roya's stomach did a flip that she promptly ignored. "Then *we* have to go to Coney Island, Stefanie," Roya said. "Maybe there's a clue."

Stefanie stared out the window at the passing cars, deep in thought. After a few moments, she said, "You're right. It's the only place to start."

"I'll just go tell Aty," Roya said, who knew her mom would let her go, especially if it was with Stefanie. Then she turned to Amin. "You're coming, right?"

"I want to," Amin said slowly. "I've been looking forward to taking the subway from here because I haven't yet." He tapped the orange *F* on his shirt. "My parents have been too busy. But . . ." His face fell. "I don't think they'd let me go without them."

"Come on," Roya said confidently as she stood up. "Let's go convince them. It'll be easy, because Stefanie"—she took Stefanie's hand and helped her up—"is a grown-up *and* a doctor."

WHEN AMIN OPENED THE DOOR to 2A, the most delicious smells wafted out into the hallway. Roya couldn't identify all the spices, but her nose picked up on turmeric, which her mom cooked with a lot too.

"That smells amazing," she told Amin.

"Our restaurant kitchen isn't fully up and running yet, so my parents are doing some of the cooking here for now," Amin explained.

"You own a restaurant?" Roya asked.

Amin nodded. "Around the corner. Taste of Bangla."

"Oh!" Stefanie said. "We saw that just opened. Katya and I were planning to go, but . . ." Her voice faded as she realized that she and Katya might not be doing *anything* they'd planned to do.

Roya took charge. "What's your last name again?" she asked Amin.

"Lahiri," Amin replied.

Roya followed the smells to the kitchen, where a man stood over an enormous pot of rice that was fogging up his glasses.

"Hi, Mr. Lahiri!" Roya said, startling the man into dropping a large metal spoon into his pot. A little bit of boiling water splashed onto his shirt.

Mr. Lahiri looked in confusion at the strange girl who had appeared in his kitchen. "Hi," he said uncertainly as he took his round, frameless glasses off to wipe away the steam.

Roya lightly pushed Amin forward so his dad could see that she had come in with his son.

"Hi, Baba," Amin said.

"Amin," Mr. Lahiri said, suddenly seeming to understand why Roya was in his apartment. "Did you make a new friend?" He said this last part eagerly.

"Yes!" Roya answered. "I'm Roya. I'm the super's kid."

"Hello, Roya," Mr. Lahiri said, smiling. "It's very nice to meet you."

Stefanie quickly stepped forward too. "Hi there. I'm Stefanie. I live in 3G. Welcome to the building."

"Thank you, Stefanie," Mr. Lahiri said. "I'm Devesh. Forgive me. I'd shake your hands, but they're not quite fit." Mr. Lahiri held up his hands, which were crusted with a red spice.

"That's quite all right," Stefanie said. "It smells incredible in here. My wife and I had just passed by your restaurant. . . ." Again, Stefanie faltered.

And again, Roya stepped in. "Mr. Lahiri, we were wondering if it would be okay for Amin to take a trip to Coney Island with us."

"Coney Island?" Mr. Lahiri asked, blinking.

"It's just a few stops on the F," Roya continued.

"Twelve stops," Amin chimed in. "We could also take the Q. But the F station is closer to here."

Mr. Lahiri looked at Amin with affection in his eyes. "I know we've been too busy to take you on the train yet. But you have food therapy today."

Roya eyed Amin curiously, wondering what exactly food therapy was. But she knew better than to ask right then, particularly as Amin glanced away at the mention of it.

"Not until five-thirty," Amin mumbled.

"Oh, we'll definitely be back before then," Roya said. "We can be back by four."

Mr. Lahiri smiled at Roya. "That's a kind offer, but, unfortunately, I'm much too busy to go with you."

"That's why Stefanie's here!" Roya said, and then added, with all the confidence she could muster—which, as her fifth-grade teacher had written on her report card, was quite a lot—"She's a doctor!"

Mr. Lahiri's lips quirked up involuntarily. "Is she now?" he said as he looked at Stefanie.

Stefanie cleared her throat. "I am. I'm a resident at New York Presbyterian. But of course I completely understand if you don't want your son getting on the subway with a couple of strangers. . . ."

"*Strangers?*" Roya asked. "No, friends! And neighbors!" She gave Stefanie a look that was meant to convey: *Don't you want our help in finding Katya?!* "Of course, we'd bring Amin back safe and sound. And if for some reason we didn't—well, you know exactly where we live."

At that, Mr. Lahiri burst into a peal of laughter. He looked over at his son.

"Please, Baba?" Amin asked in a smaller voice.

Mr. Lahiri stared at him for a moment. "As long as he can be home by four?"

"We promise," Roya said.

"Of course," Stefanie replied, nodding.

"Then have fun, Babu," he said, ruffling his son's hair.

Hello, Grandmother

ROYA SUGGESTED THEY BRING THE original lavender fortune with them, in case it held some sort of extra clue, so they grabbed it from Stefanie's apartment before heading out.

The train ride to Coney Island was almost entirely aboveground. Amin spent it with his nose pressed to the window, softly calling out the next stop just before the robotic train announcement got around to it.

"I never asked," Roya said, "but where did your family move from?"

"Sheepshead Bay," Amin said.

"Where is that exactly?" Roya asked. All she knew about that neighborhood was that it was also in Brooklyn.

"Pretty close to Coney Island, actually," Amin said.

Ah. That explained why Amin remembered the fortune-telling machine and Roya didn't. He'd probably been to Coney Island a lot more often than even she had.

"But my dad grew up in our neighborhood now," Amin continued. "Taste of Bangla used to be my grandparents' restaurant, though it hasn't been open for a few years."

Their train was now passing tall apartment buildings and a sprawling cemetery, before the track swerved them up beside the Cyclone and the Steeplechase—two large roller coasters in the center of a riot of Coney Island's bright reds, blues, and yellows. Large cartoon drawings of a man with dark, center-parted hair and a wide, red-lipped smile were dotted all around, welcoming them to the famed Luna Park. Stefanie's face was as grim as the mascot's grin was wide.

In the distance, the Atlantic Ocean sparkled in the sun like it was made of blue diamonds, and Roya squeezed Stefanie's hand. There hadn't yet been a jam she or her mom hadn't been able to find their way out of . . . not even when 4G's cat had gotten herself stuck behind the drywall of the renovations in 4H. She was confident they'd get to the bottom of this too.

"This is the last stop on this train," the conductor announced as the three of them exited the platform into the bright sunshine. They had to go down one ramp and up another to finally emerge on Surf Avenue, across from the large candy store and one of Coney Island's two Nathan's Famous hot dog shops.

"That's the original restaurant. It's over one hundred years old," Amin said softly, almost reverently, before wrinkling his nose and muttering to himself, "but the smell . . ."

Roya took a whiff: it smelled like perfectly grilled hot dogs, soft buns, and salty french fries. In other words, delicious. "You don't like hot dogs?" she asked Amin.

"Oh," Amin said, ducking his head. "No."

"Are you a vegetarian?" Roya asked curiously.

Amin shook his head. "No, just . . . I only like certain food." Roya remembered the food therapy then and was about to ask another question, when Amin changed the subject. "Look at the sign. 1916." Roya and Stefanie squinted up at the building's red and green neon lights claiming *World Famous Frankfurters Since 1916.* "That's not too long before Katya's great-great-grandmother first went to the machine, right?" Amin asked.

Stefanie nodded. "Eight years."

Roya took out her notebook and made a note of it. She couldn't see why that might be important now, but if there was one thing she'd learned from her podcast, it was that sometimes the puzzle only came into focus once you had all the pieces— even pieces you didn't know would ever fit.

CONEY ISLAND'S AMUSEMENT PARK WAS actually several parks butted up right next to each other, and in this case, the trio needed to get into Deno's Wonder Wheel Amusement Park. They walked past several kiddie rides—boats and fire trucks and rocket ships that went around in circles and that Roya had loved when she was younger—and toward the crown jewel of the park: the Wonder Wheel. Green and orange spokes held a series of metal cars, the beige ones on the outside going around in a leisurely circle, while the brightly colored ones on the inside swung wildly back and forth along the spokes like a zip line. Roya hadn't yet been able to convince either of her parents to take her on the moving cars.

"That was Charles Hermann's invention: a Ferris wheel with cars that moved," Amin explained. "I think he originally called it the perpetual motion machine. It was inspired by a da Vinci design."

Roya looked up at the wheel as she, Stefanie, and Amin walked through a brightly painted tunnel toward it. When they reached its ticket booth, Stefanie stopped suddenly and pointed out a wooden cabinet standing next to a few claw machines.

Grandmother looked smaller and kindlier than she had in Roya's imagination. She had short gray hair and a smiling, wrinkled wax face that peered down, not quite meeting the eyes of her customer. She was dressed in an old-fashioned, long-sleeved purple shirt, a gold brooch at her high collar, and a flowy, dark gray robe layered on top. A single candle with a round electric bulb stood in front of her, along with a deck of yellowing tarot cards. The rich cherry wood of the cabinet at the top simply stated: *GRANDMOTHERS PREDICTIONS*.

"That's missing an apostrophe," Amin observed.

Roya realized that all three of them were standing a bit back from the cabinet, staring in awe.

"Do you think Katya left a clue?" Roya asked.

"I don't know," Stefanie said, bleakly eyeing Grandmother's face. "She came armed with her phone and her GPS turned on. Dropped a pin on her map as soon as she got here and sent it to me. But none of it mattered." Stefanie swallowed. "Because her phone doesn't appear to be working at all now. I can't locate it." Stefanie stepped forward, looking the machine over.

Roya and Amin did the same, each silently taking a side, running their hands on the grooves of the wood, making sure there was nothing out of place. But it seemed like a perfectly ordinary novelty arcade machine. Roya asked Stefanie for the original fortune, and they carefully examined the card under the watchful gaze of Grandmother. There was nothing new to see there, either—though Roya could have sworn she caught a gleam in one of Grandmother's glass eyes.

The machine's coin slot said *50¢ Quarters Only* in a fancy font. Stefanie reached into her purse and took out the two coins, but then hesitated.

"Do you want me to do it?" Roya asked.

"No," Stefanie said. "Of course not. I couldn't bear it if anything happened to you."

"Nothing's going to happen to me. Or you, either," Roya said confidently. "Remember what Amin said? That the disappearances only happened to the Petrov daughters on the dates on the card?"

Stefanie nodded, but she still took a second before she placed the coins in Roya's outstretched hand. Roya promptly put them in the slot.

As soon as she did, Grandmother gently sprang to life, moving her hand across the deck of tarot cards in front of her. Her eyes blinked, scanning up and down from the three of them to the cards. She took a glance at the deck in her hand, gave a nod, and then spat out a thick yellow card from a slot on the right side of her cabinet.

Roya grabbed it and the three of them looked at it together.

"'I know the future has in store a great adventure once you explore,'" Amin read out loud. "'A redheaded person will prove a great friend.'" Amin looked up, blinking at Roya's dark hair and Stefanie's blue and black braids.

"I've gotten more informative fortunes from a cookie," Roya muttered. She didn't know what she'd expected, exactly, but it was definitely something more than . . . this.

She absentmindedly flipped the paper over. There was no series of dates on the back, just a generic list of lucky numbers.

But then Roya gasped. "Stefanie . . . ," she said, and thrust the card under her nose. She was pointing to some words at the bottom, in such tiny print that they could be mistaken for a copyright.

They said, in lavender ink: *You have one chance to save her.*

7

Coffee Grounds and Poetry

THEY HAD TO GET AMIN back for his therapy session, so the trio couldn't stay much longer at Coney Island, but they discussed all the information they had on the train ride back to their building.

"*How* can we save her?" Roya said. "That's the question. Where do we start?"

"Coney Island," Amin responded. "Grandmother. It's the only place *to* start. We have to come back." He looked at Stefanie for confirmation.

But Stefanie didn't seem so sure. She looked over at Roya's hands—one of them clutching the stiff yellow card they'd gotten out of the wax fortune teller's machine, and the other, the original lavender one. "Yes. Probably. But . . . I need time to think this all over."

"Of course," Roya said, nodding. She held up the two

fortunes. "Can I borrow these to look at closer? I'll be very careful with them." Stefanie nodded.

They separated after they got in the building, Stefanie going to the elevator, Amin opting to take the stairs up to his apartment, and Roya going into her apartment. She walked into the living room and past the giant wall calendar of all the plumber, electrician, painter, and other service appointments Aty had scheduled for the Queen's tenants. Out of habit, Roya waved hello to the mural of the unibrowed woman deseeding a pomegranate that Aty had painted on the wall on the opposite side. It was done in the flat style of traditional Iranian artwork, with splashes of gold leaf in the woman's veil and clothes.

Roya headed to her room, where more of Aty's artwork was painted on the wall. Here, it was two pigtailed girls flying on a magic carpet. She stared at them as she thought. She placed the two fortunes down side by side on a blank page of the journal before starting to write on the opposite page:

> How can we get Katya back?
> What sort of machine is Grandmother really?
> Is there magic involved?

She scribbled her thoughts in free-form, writing them as they came, occasionally looking at the sisters on the magic carpet for guidance and inspiration. Good investigative journalism began with asking questions, and telling a compelling story, like for a podcast, was about answering those questions. The best podcasts could unfurl the story in a way that kept the listener on the edge of their seat. Roya often used her notebook to organize her thoughts before recording, and it seemed like a good way to search for clues or patterns now too.

She kept writing until she heard the key in their front door, at which point she sprang up from her bed and out into the hallway. "Aty!"

"Hi, dokhtaram," Aty said. "How was Coney Island? Stefanie didn't seem to be feeling too much better." She had an empty tray with her, meaning that she must have taken some tea and cookies up to Stefanie, something she often did when she felt the tenants needed comfort rather than just a plumber or painter.

Aty headed to the kitchen to put on the kettle for her own cup of tea while Roya told Aty all about the train, the amusement park, and Grandmother. The double kettle was whistling by the time Roya got to the yellow card with the ominous fine print.

"We don't really know what it means," Roya said. "But Grandmother seems to be our only lead so far, so I think we have to go back to her."

"And you said Stefanie doesn't want to tell the police any of this?" Aty asked while pouring her tea in a slim glass cup.

Roya shook her head. "I think Katya's family had a bad experience with the police. Besides, it seems unlikely they'd believe her."

Aty nodded as she put a sugar cube between her teeth and sipped her tea through it. "Fortunes . . . ," she said thoughtfully.

"I know," Roya said. "I thought about that too. Maybe it's worth doing ours. In case there's a connection? Like a psychic connection?"

Aty looked at her daughter. Roya knew that most other parents would dismiss such a wild idea out of hand, or play along with their kids' fantasies despite not really believing them. But Aty was not most parents. After all, who else would have their kid call them by their first name instead of Mom?

"Why not?" Aty said now. "It's worth a try." She put down her tea and went into the kitchen, retrieving the small copper pot she used to make Turkish coffee. Then she added a spoonful of the dark, fine grounds from a container, poured in some water, and put it on the stove. While she did that, Roya went to one of their built-in bookshelves and took out the large hardcover book that sat on the bottom. Both the cover and edges of the pages were gilded in gold and decorated in a turquoise leaf pattern. The book's shimmering title, *The Divan of Hafez,* was written in both Farsi and English; Roya held it out to her mother.

"Why don't you do it?" Aty said. "After all, it's really your question."

Roya looked down at the book, running her hands over the embossed cover, the tiny leaves massaging her palm in a way that was soothing. Hafez was a fourteenth-century Persian poet, and Aty, like many people, used his book like others used tarot decks: to ask questions about decisions she had to make or things she was nervous about. Roya had also heard Aty ask a lot about Baba's health, though mostly when she thought Roya was out of earshot. Roya never stuck around to hear the responses to those questions, though. She was too afraid of them.

Roya took in a big breath now and thought about her question. What was the most important thing to ask? As curious as she was about where Katya was, they needed to *help* her. Actively. Roya could figure out exactly what had happened later, after they'd rescued her.

"How do we rescue Katya?" she said as she ran her thumbnail over the top of the book's pages and down the side, like she'd seen her mom do. Then, when the moment just *felt* right, a minuscule electric spark at the tip of her finger, she slid her thumb between the pages and opened the book.

Two short poems stared out at her, one on the left side, one on the right. She was supposed to read both and decide which one answered her question best.

The poems were written in both Farsi and English. The important lines, the ones that were supposed to tell the fortunes, were in the final couplet, the last two lines of each poem. Roya could read the English a lot better than the Farsi, despite going to Farsi school every Saturday during the school year, but even the translation was written in an old-fashioned style that made it difficult to understand.

Words stuck out at her, though. From the poem on the left, *vanished,* but from the right, something about returning through a door. Roya read the whole right-hand poem and found an even more pertinent couplet:

> *It should be asked why she left*
> *and why she came back again.*

"This one, Aty," Roya said, tapping the page. "I'm pretty sure it's this poem. Tell me what it means."

Aty took the book and read the short poem to herself. "Hmmm . . . ," she said. "The last two lines could be interpreted as something like, 'Despite breaking a promise, her grace will allow her to walk through our door again.'"

"Whose grace?" Roya asked. "Grandmother's?"

"Could be," Aty said.

"Hmph," Roya said. "That's not *very* helpful."

"Yes, well. It's a six-hundred-and-fifty-year-old book, Roya jaan, not Google Maps. It's probably not going to give you step-by-step directions," Aty quipped.

A bubbling sound informed them that the small copper pot on the stove was boiling over. Aty turned the stove off, then picked up the pot and poured the contents into a small white cup with a tiny handle. She paused as she positioned the kettle above a second cup and looked up at Roya.

"No way," Roya said. "Once was enough." Turkish coffee was thick and sludgy, and although it smelled amazing, the memory of its bitter, intense taste still made her nose wrinkle a year later.

Aty gave a small smile as she nodded and poured the drink into the second cup anyway. "I'll drink it, but this one will be your cup, and your fortune. You can turn it over when I finish."

Aty lifted the cup and took a small sip. It was too hot for her to rush, so Roya filled the silence with their usual small talk.

"How's 5J's tub?"

"All fixed," Aty said. "I just got a text that 4M's refrigerator seems to have broken down, though."

"Do I need to fill out the order form?" Roya asked.

"Already done. You were busy today, so . . ." Aty smiled at her, an assurance that she was happy that Roya was too busy doing regular kid things—well, as much as figuring out why a tenant disappeared and what it had to do with a hundred-year-old fortune-telling machine could be considered *regular.* "Your baba was feeling a little better today," Aty offered pointedly, taking another sip of the coffee.

"Oh," Roya said. "That's good. Oh, hey, do we need to call the dump truck about picking up the old refrigerator?" Roya could chat to her mom about practically anything . . . anything except her podcast or her dad. The podcast was because as much as Aty seemed to treasure giving Roya her independence, she took nothing as seriously as her job, and Roya doubted she'd be pleased about having her tenants' dirty laundry aired— sometimes literally, as in the case of 6K's unimaginably stinky socks taking a washing machine out of commission for two days. As for her dad, well, it was for the same reason she couldn't stick around to listen to what *The Divan of Hafez* had to say about what would happen to him. The bad news, the worst news, was so very bad that she didn't think she could ever stand to hear it.

"Already did that too," Aty said. She was clearly not going to let Roya change the subject completely, though, because she added, "And let's figure out when you're going to visit Baba next."

Visiting Baba required a lot of preparation. He was immuno-compromised, so Roya had to be as sanitized as possible, as well as wear a face mask. But that's not why she avoided it, really. It was because seeing him like that, so skinny and lying in bed . . . it was starting to creep up over the other memories she had of him, like weeds overtaking a garden. The memory of him sweet-talking the ride attendant at the pirate ship at Luna Park so they could go together even though she was one inch too short? Now she could only hear his voice as the weaker, raspier version she'd been listening to over the past year. Or the memory of being spun around in a circle, her dad's strong arms grasping her own so that her legs flew off the ground? His arms were skinnier than hers now. Worst of all, the last time Roya saw him, she had actually watched him lose his balance and fall, all while simply getting up from his chair. That's probably why she'd been putting off this latest visit for longer than usual.

"Okay," Roya said reluctantly.

"Check the calendar." Aty pointed to the large wall calendar where Baba's chemotherapy appointments were written in green ink. Roya had to time her visits to be in the window between ten and twenty-one days after his latest session, which was the safest time for both his immune system and his energy level.

"I will," Roya said without looking over at the calendar. She pointed to Aty's cup. "Are you done yet?"

"Almost," Aty said as she took one last gulp. "There." She placed a saucer on the lip of the cup and handed it over to Roya. "Now turn it toward your heart."

Roya took the saucer and cup with her left hand, placing her thumb on top of the saucer and flipping the whole thing over to set it on the table. They had to wait a few minutes for the thick coffee at the bottom to drip into the saucer and form the shapes that Aty would try to interpret. While they did, Aty picked up her own journal and started doodling in it while Roya picked up hers and jotted down Aty's interpretation of Hafez's poem. The scratching of their respective pencils was the only sound in the room for a few minutes.

Until Roya finally asked, impatiently, "You think it's ready?"

"Let's see," Aty said as she lifted the coffee cup and tilted it toward herself. Some of the liquid had pooled in the saucer, but there was a good amount left at the bottom and sides of the cup. Aty slowly turned it to look at the shapes and patterns that remained. Roya peeked over her shoulder.

"It looks like two people holding hands, doesn't it?" Aty said as she pointed out two figures near the edge of the cup.

"Kinda," Roya admitted. "Maybe Stefanie and Katya?"

"Maybe," Aty said. "Though something about them feels . . . younger. Like kids."

"Hey, look at this!" Roya said, pointing out a large, circular shape behind the two figures. "Doesn't that look like the Wonder Wheel?"

Aty nodded. "You're right."

"That seems like a good sign!" Roya said hopefully. "That we'll solve this and reunite Stefanie and Katya."

"I hope so," Aty agreed.

8
The Place That Never Disappoints

"**AND SO, THE GREAT CLOG** has been unclogged. The culprit? A linty, old blanket Sir Leaksalot chose to hand-wash in the bathtub. Join us next week as we look into Mrs. Hauntedface's porcelain dolls. Are they possessed or simply from the imagination of a deeply disturbed dollmaker?"

Roya would have to record that last line again since it was interrupted by a knock at her front door. She turned off her recorder and waited for whichever tenant was there to finish talking to her mom. She was surprised when Aty called out that the visitor was for her.

Roya came out from her bedroom just in time to see Aty leading a shy-looking Amin into their living room.

"Hey!" Roya said enthusiastically.

"Hey," Amin said quietly, looking off at the bright red pomegranate seeds in Aty's mural. "I hope this is okay, to show up here like this. I just thought since neither of us have phones . . ."

"Of course it's okay!" Roya said. "It's like what kids must have done in the olden days to communicate: knocking on each other's doors!"

Roya heard Aty give a faint snort and realized she'd never formally introduced them to one another. "Aty, this is Amin. Amin, this is my mom, Aty. I'm sure she's been up to your apartment to check in on your parents and your move."

"Yes, she has," Amin said.

Aty smiled warmly at Amin. "And how is everyone settling in?"

"Good," Amin replied.

"Glad to hear it. Make sure your parents know they can come to me if they need anything. Roya jaan, I'm going to the basement to bag the recyclables." Normally, Roya would go with her, but Aty's winking reminder to "Have fun. Don't do anything I wouldn't do" confirmed that her mom didn't expect her to today.

A second after Aty had shut the front door, Roya turned to Amin and said, "Nice shirt!" Amin's black T-shirt sported the letter G in a light green circle.

"Thanks," Amin said.

"You had the F train on yesterday, right?"

"Yes," Amin said.

"Do you wear them in order or something?"

"Yes." Amin sounded a little surprised. "You noticed that?"

Roya shrugged. "I'm pretty good with picking up details. Plus I've been training myself to get even better at it. I want to be an investigative journalist."

"Oh! Cool," Amin said as he lightly touched his shirt. He seemed to hesitate for just a second before he added, "Wearing the shirts in order sort of . . . I don't know, helps me feel like I have a sense of control even if things around me aren't controllable."

Roya took that in and racked her brain. There was no H or I train in the New York City subway system. "So tomorrow's is the J?"

Amin grinned. "Exactly. It was pretty amazing to be wearing the F while on the F train yesterday. It's rare when that happens. I think of those as lucky days."

"We could take the G today! Since they both come to our stop," Roya said. "Though the G doesn't go to Coney Island."

"True," Amin said. "And anyway, my parents won't let me take the train without a responsible adult, and they're both too busy today. Stefanie's not here, either. I saw her leave with some of our other neighbors who suggested they flyer the area with Missing posters of Katya."

"Ah," Roya said. Aty would let her take the train by herself, though that probably wouldn't help Amin since she doubted his parents would count her as *a responsible adult*. "Well, maybe there's something else we could do to help Katya."

"My thoughts exactly," Amin said.

"Yesterday, Aty and I tried out some fortune-telling of our own," Roya shared. "To see if we could get a clue of where to start."

"Fortune-telling?" Amin asked.

Roya nodded. "Through coffee grounds. And this book of Persian poetry." She pointed in the direction of the bookcase.

"Oh," Amin said. "Did it help?"

"Not really," Roya admitted. "I mean, it was vague."

Amin nodded seriously. "That seems to be the problem with fortune-telling. I've been disappointed by many cookies in my life."

Roya couldn't help but smile. "I guess everyone has a disappointing cookie every now and again."

"There is someplace we could look for clues," Amin said. "Someplace that rarely disappoints me."

"Where's that?" Roya asked.

A cloud must have just departed from in front of the sun, because the light from the window splayed across Amin's face, turning his large brown eyes amber and gold as he said, "The library."

AMIN'S PARENTS WOULDN'T LET HIM walk to the library without an adult, either, but his mother did agree to drop them off. Mrs. Lahiri was dressed in a dark blue tunic and pants, with silver thread that shimmered in the hot summer sun. Her headscarf was in opposite colors: silver with a floral design of blue thread.

"Wow," Roya said. "You look very glamorous."

She laughed. "I work front-of-house at the restaurant, so I have to be somewhat presentable."

"What does that mean?" Roya asked.

"It means she seats the guests and runs things in the dining room," Amin explained. "My dad is the head chef in the kitchen. That's called back-of-house."

Mrs. Lahiri nodded, beaming at her son. When they got to the library, she looked at the delicate silver watch on her wrist that—naturally—matched the rest of her outfit. "Two hours is good? I can pick you up during my break."

Amin nodded. "That should work, Ma. See you then."

Mrs. Lahiri kissed Amin on the head and gave a friendly wave to Roya. She stood on the sidewalk and waited until she was sure they had walked into the building before setting off on the two blocks that would take her to work.

Their local library branch was small and uncrowded at this

hour of the morning. Amin found his way to the small Brooklyn history section.

"What are we looking for?" Roya said as she stared at the three shelves of books.

"Let's start with anything on Coney Island and go from there," Amin said with confidence. "Maybe we can find out something about Grandmother."

They wound up pulling three books about Coney Island and another that was a collection of old photographs of Brooklyn dating back more than a hundred years. Amin brought them over to a desk by a computer and asked Roya if she'd mind browsing through them while he looked up census records.

Roya thumbed quickly through the books, at first just keeping an eye out for anything related to Grandmother. But she soon found herself slowing down to examine familiar places and landmarks. There was Grand Army Plaza, only in grainy black and white with no farmers market to be seen. And there was a photo of the Prospect Park Carousel in mid-construction.

"Hey! That's our building!" she said when she found a picture of Ocean Parkway, carts and horses running along the wide street, while people in top hats and fancy updos were riding bicycles on the sidewalk. She read the caption. " 'The country's first bike lane.' Just like you said."

Amin nodded, looking pleased with himself.

Roya continued reading, getting lost in learning about the history of familiar locations. She'd almost forgotten what they were looking for in the first place until a passage jumped out at her. "Look! It's a paragraph about Grandmother," Roya said, pointing it out. "It says she was probably built in 1929 and has been 'the Guardian of the Wonder Wheel' since then. The owners of Coney Island were under strict instructions never to separate her from the Wheel. Although, hmmm . . . what year did Stefanie say that Natasha went there?"

"One hundred years ago," Amin said, looking down at the piece of paper that he'd been working on the whole time. "Which doesn't match up exactly. But that's not surprising. Even history books don't get everything right all the time."

Roya frowned, looking back at her passage. If they couldn't trust the reporting here, then how could this help them? She glanced over at Amin to see what he had been working on and gasped. His diagram was a thing of beauty. He'd been drawing on two pieces of paper taped together—Roya had wondered why he'd asked the librarian for tape but had been too absorbed in her own book to find out the answer—and it was filled to the brim with information. It had meticulous boxes and tiny, neat handwriting depicting Katya's entire family tree dating back over a hundred years ago to when Natasha and Ivan arrived at

Ellis Island. But there were other notes in there too. Notes about what was happening in Brooklyn, the country, and sometimes even the world at large during the depicted timeline. Roya felt like a slacker in comparison.

"I thought I'd show this to Stefanie and see if she can fill in any of the gaps," Amin said.

"There are gaps?" Roya asked.

"I'm sure," Amin replied. "This was all I could get out of the official records. But plenty of things don't make it into the records. Or even history books." He sounded wistful when he said it, like it was a hard truth he'd had to accept. Then he glimpsed his mother walking through the library's front door and told Roya, "Let's check these books out and get back to headquarters."

Headquarters. Roya grinned. She liked the sound of that. It was way more exciting than simply going home.

The Only Lead

"THIS IS ASTONISHING," STEFANIE SAID as she looked at Amin's chart. Roya and Amin had cornered her with their discoveries as soon as she'd walked into the building, and she had invited them up to her apartment straightaway.

"I know, right?" Roya agreed.

Amin blushed. "It's just information that's out there," he said. "It's not like I discovered anything new."

"It's probably more useful than anything I did today," Stefanie said with a frustrated sigh. "It's so kind of our neighbors to want to help, but I just know wherever Katya is, it's not reachable via flyers. Even if putting them up gave me something to do for a few hours." Stefanie looked sad as she peered at Amin's paper more closely.

"Do you see anything in there that's inaccurate?" Amin asked. "Or do you have any information you can add?"

"Well, I know for a fact that Natasha visited Grandmother in 1924. So this must be wrong," Stefanie said, pointing at the sentence that claimed that Grandmother was built in 1929 with a question mark next to it.

"I agree," Amin replied.

"Do you think you might be able to give us copies of some of their photos, Stefanie?" Roya asked, pointing at Katya's family albums that they'd splayed out on the coffee table. "Natasha, Polina, Annika, Daria, and, I guess, Katya?" Stefanie flinched at hearing her wife's name at the end of a list of people who had disappeared for good, so Roya quickly added, "It might just help to have pictures to go along with the information."

Stefanie collected herself before she said softly, "Yes, of course. I can print some copies of the photos."

"When do you think we can go back to Coney Island?" Amin asked. "Tomorrow?"

Stefanie turned her warm brown eyes to Amin. "Do you think we'd get anything more out of it than we already have?"

"I think it's still our biggest lead," Roya said.

"And maybe something we discovered here will have more significance now," Amin added.

"Maybe . . . ," Stefanie said, staring off into space. Roya could see she was struggling with the thought of returning to the place where her wife had disappeared. But then she seemed to gather herself up. "Of course we should go back," she said in a businesslike tone. "I'm meeting with the police again tomorrow and we're short-staffed at the hospital, so I have some shifts to work this weekend. But how about Monday?"

"My schedule's very, very open," Roya said playfully.

"Mine too," Amin added in a more serious tone.

"Okay," Stefanie said. "As long as your parents okay it too, then I'll meet you in the lobby on Monday. Ten a.m."

"COMING UP, WHY IS GRANDMOTHER known as the Guardian of the Wheel? And is that *all* she's guarding? Right after a word from our sponsors." Roya pressed pause on her recorder. Technically, *QOOP* didn't have sponsors yet, but she always liked to record a transition just in case it ever did.

She took her tablet, her tenth-birthday present from her parents, and navigated over to her podcast's landing page. Still forty-seven subscribers, just like yesterday, over half of them from—for some unknown reason—Denmark. ("I'm huge in Denmark," she liked to joke when she was pretending she was being interviewed for a late-night show.) Only a few of *QOOP*'s subscribers were from the US at all, and none were from New York, which meant that, as far as Roya knew, no one she'd met in real life had ever listened to her podcast. This was just how she liked it. After all, she spent every episode talking about the people in her building. Even if they had made-up names, she was pretty sure that Ms. Gordon in 2C, for example, would recognize herself as Ms. Glitterkitty, aka the person who puts on a sparkly pink jumpsuit to walk her cat.

Roya wondered if her subscriber number would change once she'd posted Katya's episode, which seemed bigger and more complex than anything she'd ever produced. But, of course, she could only post it if Katya were found.

No, not *if*. *When*, she firmly told herself just as she got a FaceTime notification. Baba.

She took in a deep breath, exchanged the grimace on her face for a smile, and pressed the accept button right before the call was about to drop off.

"Hi, Baba."

"Azizam," he said. "How are you?"

"I'm good," she said automatically. There was a pause, probably right where her own question of *How are you* would go. But she didn't ask, because she didn't want to hear it: not the truth and not the lie that Baba would inevitably tell instead.

"*Are* you good?" Baba asked suspiciously, and Roya noticed he wasn't smiling back at her, a rarity. Roya shifted uncomfortably, bracing herself for more bad news. "I heard about Katya going missing. I can't believe it. It's so terrible," Baba said.

Roya was relieved, even though she also immediately felt guilty about it. Still, it was some comfort that Baba's grim face wasn't about different bad news, just the bad news she was already working on.

"Yes," she said. "It *is* terrible. But Amin and I are trying to help Stefanie. Amin's my new friend. He just moved into 2A." Roya spent the next few minutes filling her dad in on everything she and Amin had learned about Katya's family and Grandmother's Predictions.

In another lifetime—which was, in fact, just last year—Payman Alborzi was a high school physics teacher at Bronx Science. He had taken a sabbatical that was meant to last for only a few months but had been extended longer and longer as his treatments had. But even if he wasn't teaching, Baba would always be a scientist at heart, and so he listened carefully to everything Roya said, asking questions only once he had processed all the information she had to share.

"So you want to go back to Grandmother?" he asked.

Roya nodded. "It's the only place that's given us any clues: both the fortune from 1924 and the one from this week. Seems like the logical next step."

Baba had a faraway look in his eye. It was his thinking-grand-theoretical-thoughts face, and Roya felt a surge of hope blossom in her chest at the sight of it. She hadn't seen that look in a while, but it was so quintessentially her dad that, for a moment, it overtook the gauntness of his features and the plastic port in his chest, just visible at the bottom of the video frame. "I would agree," he said. "Promise to keep me posted on what you find?"

"Of course," Roya said with a smile, feeling better after a conversation with her dad instead of worse, which was something she hadn't been able to say for a long time.

10

A Manifestation

MONDAY MORNING WAS GRAY, THE sky so flat that it looked like a backdrop. If you peered closely, you could see the edges of the large clouds that were covering up the sun.

"It looks like rain," Stefanie said as she stepped off the elevator and peeked outside the building's large glass doors.

She walked back into the elevator, and for a split second, Roya worried that she was going to cancel the trip. But then she said, "Be right back," and in less than a minute, she returned to the lobby with a couple of umbrellas. On their way to the subway station, they passed some of the flyers of Katya's face that Stefanie and their neighbors must have put up last week.

Their train ride was quiet, the cars almost empty as it was too ominous a day for the seashore. Two stops in, someone got on eating a pungent bacon-and-egg sandwich, and Amin, looking queasy, asked if they'd mind changing cars.

Once they settled into their new seats, Amin started reading through one of the Coney Island books he and Roya had gotten from the library. Roya had brought her journal and was looking over a draft segment of Katya's podcast episode. Stefanie was staring off into the distance, lost in unhappy thoughts. They passed above the large cemetery, looking even grayer and sadder than usual in the weak sunlight, and Roya had to fight hard to stop her mind from going to the dark place it did when things felt so heavy.

She would not picture Baba's name on one of those stones. She would *not*.

"Anything interesting in your book?" Roya asked Amin, breaking up her own thoughts.

"There's *plenty* interesting in here," Amin said.

"Right," Roya said. "But anything related to what we're doing? Grandmother?"

"Nothing obvious," Amin admitted. "But there is a lot of cool stuff about the Wonder Wheel. In that passage you found last week, Grandmother was called the Guardian of the Wheel, right?"

"Right," Roya said.

"Well, the Wonder Wheel has been in operation for over a hundred years. And apparently Deno, the guy whose name is on it now, bought it in the 1980s. He'd proposed to his wife on it when he was just a hot dog vendor, and he didn't have a ring, so he promised he'd buy the Wheel for her one day."

"Huh," Roya said. "Like a manifestation?" Aty had told her about those. How if you wanted something, sometimes you had to visualize it actually happening to you. It helped to say it aloud, write it down, or even express gratitude to the universe as if it had already happened.

"Or maybe like a romantic gesture," Stefanie murmured, a small, sad smile on her face. "I proposed to Katya at Coney Island too. On the beach. She loves the ocean."

"Oh," Roya said. She really didn't know much about romance. But manifestation might actually be helpful here. She closed her eyes, tried to wipe out all other thoughts, and imagined the three of them finding Katya on the boardwalk. Today. Underneath all the low-hanging clouds. She even pictured the sky breaking open and dousing them with large, fat rain droplets like confetti.

WHEN THEY GOT OFF THE train, they walked in near silence past the first Nathan's, up the ramp to the boardwalk, and to the entrance of Deno's Wonder Wheel Amusement Park. Roya saw Stefanie staring wistfully once or twice out toward the ocean. *We'll find her,* Roya said in her mind. *Today.*

By the time they made it down the large, colorful ramp that led to the Wonder Wheel, small raindrops were prickling their skin.

"We might not have much time," Amin said. "They'll probably close the park if it starts raining too hard."

Roya led the way to Grandmother. Once again, the wax figure looked small and unassuming.

"I guess . . . let's try another fortune?" Roya asked.

Amin nodded. He pushed aside the hem of his T-shirt, the Q train one today, to pluck two quarters from his pocket. He handed them over to Roya, who put them into the slot and turned the knob.

The sky darkened, just for a moment. Not like a cloud passing over the sun, but as if the whole blue expanse had suddenly been switched off like a TV screen. Only it was so quick that Roya wasn't sure whether it had actually happened or if she'd just blinked.

But after the moment of absolute darkness, everything was bright. Blindingly bright. It was suddenly a gorgeous sunny day, not a cloud in the sky. The temperature had increased at least ten degrees.

"What in the heck?" Roya asked. Amin was next to her, looking just as baffled. She turned around to see if Stefanie was as confused as they were.

But Stefanie wasn't there.

That didn't make sense. She had been right behind them. And it wasn't like the park was crowded on a rainy Monday morning.

Only that wasn't true. The park was suddenly swarming. There were families and couples and *people* in every corner.

"Where did everyone come from?" Roya wondered aloud.

She turned to Amin, but he was staring at one of the brick walls behind them. "Those weren't there when we got here," he said. He was pointing at a few flyers advertising a food truck festival that was taking place on the boardwalk over the weekend. *Wait, no.* It was last weekend.

Amin went to take a closer look at the flyers, and Roya followed. She hadn't noticed them one way or another, and though she trusted in Amin's acute powers of observation, she was about to tell him that it seemed like less of a concern than the sudden about-face in weather and crowd size. But then something in her peripheral vision caught her eye: it was a lavender scarf billowing in the light breeze. It was being used as a headband on a blond head—a blond head that looked familiar.

Roya gasped. "Katya!" she said, pointing at the woman who stood in front of Grandmother's machine. Her hand was near the coin slot, as if she had just put the quarters in. Grandmother was moving her own wax hands over the tarot cards. Roya couldn't believe it. The manifestation had worked.

Amin's attention moved away from the flyers and toward Katya. Grandmother had stopped moving, and Katya was bending down to retrieve her fortune.

Roya glimpsed the lavender card that Katya was removing before she and Amin both yelled out in unison, "Katya!"

Katya turned to them, a look of surprise on her face. There was a flash of recognition as she caught sight of Roya.

And then, suddenly, she was gone. Vanished right before their eyes.

11

Back and Forth

ROYA AND AMIN STARED AT each other for a split second before running through a large family that was clearly about to get in line for the Wonder Wheel. When they got back to Grandmother, they searched the area around her cabinet, looking for signs of Katya, even though they both knew what had happened: they had literally watched her *disappear.*

"What's going on?" Roya asked. "What do we do?"

"I think," Amin said slowly, touching the side of Grandmother's cabinet, "we might need to put coins in. To go back or . . ." He looked off at the food truck festival flyers again. "Maybe forward?"

"What are you talking about?" Roya asked as a couple of teenagers came up to them.

"Excuse me?" one asked. "Are you using this?"

Roya turned to Amin for an answer, since he seemed to have more of a grasp on what was going on than she did.

"No, not yet," Amin said, and indicated to Roya that they should step away from the machine. "Let's watch them," he whispered.

So they did, Roya jotting notes in her journal and thinking in her narrator voice because it helped her catch more details.

The first teen, dressed almost head to toe in black, puts in her two quarters. The other teen, looking bored, tells her friend to . . .

And this is where, if she'd been recording them, Roya would patch in their actual voices saying:

TEEN 2: Hurry up. The line for the Cyclone keeps getting longer.

TEEN 1: I just want to know if it's going to tell me anything about Ronan.

TEEN 2: If it doesn't, I will. Just ask him out. And then you'll have your answer. A real one. Not "all signs point to yes" or whatever.

Grandmother's card comes out of the slot, and the black-clad teen bends over to pick it up. Her face falls as she reads it.

TEEN 1: "What you seek, you'll never find, if your intended never knows your mind."

TEEN 2: Ha! See?! I told you! Thanks, Grammy!

TEEN 1: But I can't just ask him! Not without knowing if he'll say yes.

Roya watched them leave, curious about how that story would end, but when she turned around to ask Amin about it, he was already back at the cabinet. Roya shook her head and reminded herself to focus on the much more important mystery at hand.

"I think we have to put quarters in too," Amin was saying. "I only hope . . ." He looked off worriedly in the direction where the two teens had disappeared into the crowd.

"Only hope what?" asked Roya.

"Well. That we have better luck than them. Or maybe *luck* is not the right word." Amin reached into his pocket and took out two quarters from his stash.

He put one in and then reached for Roya's hand. "Ready?" he asked.

Roya wasn't sure exactly what she was ready for, but she nodded anyway, taking Amin's hand as he put in the second quarter.

As soon as she heard the coin clink into the cabinet's internal mechanisms, there was another flash of darkness, another blip. But this time, when the world turned back on, it was no longer bright and sunny. The gray clouds had returned, and what's more, they'd actually opened up. A steady drizzle fell upon their heads.

"Oh, thank goodness!" a frantic voice came from behind them. They turned around to see Stefanie, who rushed forward and gave them both a tight hug. Then she held each of them away and examined them from head to toe, even checking their pulses with her two fingers. "Maybe I'm losing my mind."

"What happened?" Amin asked.

"You . . . ," Stefanie started, sounding like she was on the verge of tears. "Well, you're not going to believe this. But it's like you two disappeared. And then just appeared again."

"Oh, we believe you," Amin said.

"You do?" Stefanie asked, blinking.

Roya nodded. "Yes. Because we just saw the same thing happen to Katya."

"You saw Katya?" Stefanie said, spinning around in a circle. "Where?"

"She's not here. Or at least, she's not now," Amin said as he pointed to the brick wall just ahead of them. This time, Roya noticed it too: no flyers.

"I don't understand," Stefanie said.

"I think . . . ," Amin said, looking at the blank wall. "I think . . . we traveled back in time."

An Impossible Theory

ROYA AND STEFANIE BOTH STARED at Amin in shock.

"In time?" Roya asked blankly. "Are you sure?"

"How else would you explain it?" Amin replied. "The weather. The flyers. Katya herself. It's the only thing that makes sense."

But of course it didn't make sense. People couldn't travel in time . . . could they? Changing weather and a missing flyer probably had a more likely explanation than *time travel*.

Roya looked over at Stefanie, expecting her to echo her rational thoughts. Instead, Stefanie seemed to be stuck on something else entirely. "You really saw her? Katya?"

Amin nodded.

"You're sure it was her?" Stefanie asked.

Amin glanced at Roya for confirmation. "Yes," Roya said. "It was her. She even turned at the sound of her name."

"Let's go try again," Stefanie said, walking over to Grandmother. "You just put the coins in and then you traveled, right?" Amin nodded again.

Roya was astounded. Did *Doctor* Stefanie Turner actually believe Amin's theory? "Do you really think we time-traveled, Stefanie?" she had to ask.

"I don't know what to think," Stefanie admitted as she put a hand on Grandmother's cabinet. "But if you two say you saw her, I believe you. So we have to try and go again. Together."

"That makes sense," Roya admitted.

This was getting exciting. If they really *were* traveling in time, then she needed to gather more careful observations of what it all felt like, sounded like, looked like. What could be the title of this episode? *The Time-Traveling Fortune Teller?* Or *Grandmother: A Portal Through Time?* Or . . . maybe she'd work on the title later.

"Let's do it," Stefanie said. Amin handed her two quarters from his pocket. Stefanie put one in.

"Should we hold hands?" Amin asked. "Maybe we need to all be touching in order to go together."

They grasped each other's hands. "Ready?" Stefanie asked, and the kids nodded. Stefanie plopped the other coin in. Roya waited with bated breath as it clinked through the machine's chutes and passages. She kept her eyes wide open, prepared for the blip this time.

But nothing happened.

Well, that wasn't entirely true. Grandmother moved her hands robotically, and she shot out one of her usual yellow fortunes. So *something* happened. But certainly nothing that could be considered a breach in the space-time continuum.

And there was nothing special about the fortune, either. It said, *Early to bed, early to rise, wouldn't make a night owl very wise,* and was completely blank on the other side.

Still, Stefanie was frantically searching around, obviously looking for Katya.

"I don't think she's here." Roya broke the news gently. "This isn't what it felt like before."

Amin shook his head. "But Roya put the coins in last time. Maybe she needs to again?"

Stefanie nodded. "Okay. Let's try that."

Roya took Amin's coins. Her stomach seemed to drop with each one she inserted into the slot, her other hand wet from rain and sweat as it held on to Amin's.

But again, nothing extraordinary happened.

For good measure, they tried it with Amin putting the coins in too, and received their third yellow fortune card of the day: *Your mind is your map, but the compass is your heart. Don't overthink to know where to start.*

"Do you think this is a clue?" Amin asked.

Roya read it and shrugged. "Sounds like something Aty would say. 'Always trust your gut,' basically. Is your gut telling you something?"

"Not really," Amin said, looking deep into Grandmother's glass eyes, as if she might have the answer. "Except that maybe we can only travel at certain times. Or it can only happen once a day," he mumbled.

Stefanie stared at Grandmother a moment too, before saying, "Either way, it's getting late. And this rain doesn't seem to be letting up. I think we should probably head home." Her face was a mixture of puzzled and troubled as she peered into the cabinet.

"But we just saw Katya," Roya said. "Maybe there are other combinations we can try."

To Roya's surprise, Amin agreed with Stefanie. "Stefanie's right. I don't have many quarters left. Besides, I think we should do some more research before we come back."

Research? Roya was incredulous. How could something in a dusty book compare to what they'd just experienced? The library was cool and all, but it didn't measure up to having an actual adventure. But Amin and Stefanie had already started to walk away. Roya looked longingly at the cabinet one more time.

She gave Grandmother a small salute and whispered, "We'll be back," before following Stefanie and Amin out of Deno's Park.

AMIN SPENT THE MORNING AT the library while Roya helped her mom out with letting in and taking care of the construction crew working on turning apartment 6J into two smaller apartments. She also recorded a few segments for her podcast, trying to describe some of the sensations she and Amin had experienced yesterday. She vowed to remember to bring her voice recorder next time they visited Grandmother. Which also meant it might be time to let Amin in on her big secret.

When Amin got back from the library, he told Roya that he didn't find out too much. "Time travel is complicated. And mostly theoretical," he admitted.

"So . . . maybe we didn't travel back in time?" Roya asked.

"Maybe," Amin said. "Either way, I think we should go back as soon as we can. And try to re-create some of the same circumstances."

"Okay," Roya said. "I have something to tell you too." She navigated over to the landing page of her podcast.

"Whoa!" Amin said, checking out the titles, including "2C: Ms. Glitterkitty" and "1H: The Case of the Haunted Dolls." "These are about our neighbors?"

Roya nodded. "I think I should bring my recorder next time we go to Coney Island. Even if we never post this episode, it's a really good way to keep track of what we learn so we don't miss anything."

"Definitely," Amin said enthusiastically as he looked at the landing page again. "Can I listen to these sometime?"

"Sure," Roya said. "But don't tell anyone around here about the podcast. I'm going to tell Stefanie that the recorder is just to help us out with possible clues."

Amin looked a little worried but then nodded. "Okay."

THE NEXT DAY, STEFANIE CALLED out of work so that they could return to Coney Island.

It was a warm, pleasant day, and the place was much busier than on a rainy Monday. They had to wait in line to even get to Grandmother. When they finally stood in front of her, Roya pressed a button on her recorder, and they starting going through their quarters. Amin and Roya had raided everything their families had set aside for the laundry room, including Aty's rather large stash that she used to make change for the other residents. Stefanie had gotten rolls of coins from the bank.

They tried every combination of inserting the coins they could think of.

Amin had even worn his Q train shirt again, just in case that had something to do with it. He'd estimated the time they'd gone, down to within ten minutes, and for those ten minutes, they relentlessly put in coin after coin, even when there were people standing behind them. It got to the point that the others waiting in line finally left, grumbling about taking turns and rudeness.

Stefanie ignored it; they all did. This was too important. And besides, maybe if strangers thought they were a little kooky, they would *want* to keep their distance and they'd get Grandmother all to themselves.

Two hours after they arrived, they were all out of coins and had traveled absolutely nowhere—through neither space nor time.

"I don't think it's going to work." Roya finally voiced what they'd all been thinking for at least the past twenty minutes.

Stefanie and Amin had to agree. "Maybe it was too big of a reach," Stefanie said dejectedly after Roya had stopped recording and they were walking back toward the subway, their mood somber. "After all, time travel isn't really possible."

"But you *do* believe we saw Katya, right?" Roya asked.

Stefanie hesitated for only a moment but then said firmly, "I do believe you. I just don't know how."

"I'm going to do more research tomorrow," Amin said.

"I'll go with you," Stefanie replied. "Do you think your parents will let you come to the main branch of the library with me? We might find a lot more information there."

Amin's eyes gleamed. "Oh, yes. I think they would!"

Stefanie turned to Roya. "And Aty will definitely let *you*."

But Roya's heart sank. "Can't. I, uh . . . have to go see my dad." She had finally picked the day on the calendar, and she couldn't put it off again. Not even for something as important as trying to find Katya.

Stefanie just nodded. "We'll keep you posted on anything we find."

A Tale of Two Corneliuses

ROYA HAD BEEN PUTTING OFF the latest visit with her dad for so long that Baba was due to go back in the hospital for another round of chemotherapy the next day. The hospital was an all-day affair that Roya tried very hard to keep herself occupied for. Aty was the one who would take Baba, so she was gone for most of the day, leaving Roya to eagerly take over her duties as de facto super. The more tasks and complaints and leaky ceilings she could manage, the better.

Tomorrow, she could throw herself into the mystery of the (maybe) time-traveling fortune-telling machine. But for today, she'd have to put on two masks: the protective surgical one and the smile underneath it that pretended she was just as cheerful seeing her dad eight pounds thinner than when she last saw him. The smile would be attached to a mouth that could happily natter on about whatever silly thing had happened at school, when it was still in session, or in the building. She would talk and talk and talk, and he would listen and chuckle, and then they'd play whatever new episodes their favorite podcast had dropped. They both pretended that filling the space with noise would push out the giant truth that was in there with them, trying to suck out all the air like an aggressive vacuum cleaner. Or a black hole.

But when she got to her dad's apartment today, bringing his favorite gummy cherries as a gift, she was happy she had a genuinely involved topic to discuss: Katya.

Baba's apartment was in Bay Ridge. It was the one he had grown up in with his uncle Khosrow. Baba was just a baby when his parents had passed away and Amoo Khosrow had been appointed his guardian, bringing him over from Iran to the US, where Khosrow already lived. Amoo Khosrow had gifted the apartment to Baba and Aty as a wedding present, but they had rented it out to tenants once Aty got her job at the Queen. Baba had moved back in after their divorce, so Roya only had about a year of memories in here that weren't tainted with Baba's illness.

Today, Roya was cheered to find Baba in the living room, as opposed to the bedroom, where they'd spent her last few visits. It was a good sign when Baba was able to get out of bed and dress in something other than pajamas. He'd even put some carrots and dip out for her today. He'd barely asked Roya how she was doing when Roya blurted out, "I saw Katya yesterday!"

"What?" Baba asked, startled. "Aty didn't tell me she'd been found."

That was partially because Roya hadn't updated Aty yet. But also because: "Well, Katya hasn't been *found*. Not exactly." For the next half hour, Roya went on to detail everything she could remember about their recent trips to Coney Island.

"Wow," Baba said when she was all done. "Wow."

"Do you believe Amin's theory? That it might be time travel?" Baba had opened up the gummy cherries and politely taken one, but Roya herself had eaten nearly half the bag already. She took another one now and bit into it, putting her mask back up while she chewed.

"First of all, I think maybe that's enough candy for today. Have a carrot?" Baba said mildly.

Roya nodded, a smile playing at her lips as she put down the bag and picked up a vegetable. Any day her dad was feeling well enough to say dad-like things was a pretty good day.

"And secondly . . ." Baba sat back in his chair and thought. "Well, there are so many things in this world we just don't know anything about. Things that a hundred years from now will be common knowledge, but are unfathomable to us now. Do you know when I was growing up, we didn't even have the internet? It didn't exist yet!"

Roya smiled. She knew this already, but it felt nice to have a normal, non-stilted conversation with her father where she wasn't actively trying so hard to avoid any talk of illness. Or as normal as a conversation about time-traveling amusement park curiosities could be. "So you think time travel doesn't exist yet?"

"Not exactly," Baba said. "Maybe that was the wrong analogy. Maybe it's more like the theory of gravity. Gravity itself existed before Isaac Newton wrote about it. But that's how everyone else came to know about it too. I think if time travel is possible, it's like that. We're still trying to figure it out." Baba was sounding more and more like the scientist Roya knew. Roya settled into that feeling like sinking into a familiar, cushy couch.

"So what you're saying is that just because no one has proven it yet," Roya interpreted, "it doesn't mean time travel is not possible."

"Exactly," Baba said, nodding. "That's exactly it. Einstein's theory of relativity—you know that famous one, E equals MC-squared—sort of blew the possibility of time travel wide open. Because, basically, he discovered that the theory of—"

"Wait," Roya said. "Do you mind if I record this? It might help if I play it for Amin." She was also thinking about her podcast, of course, but she didn't tell Baba that.

Baba smiled as he recognized his and Aty's birthday gift to their daughter. "Go right ahead, azizam." He waited for Roya to hit the red button before he repeated what he'd said about Einstein's formula and went on to explain, "The formula basically says that space and time are connected. And that gravity and mass can warp the space–time continuum. Meaning the faster you move through space, the slower you move through time. But we're talking really fast, like light-year fast."

"I'm not sure I understand," Roya admitted.

"Let's pretend there's a spaceship that could fly at the speed of light," Baba said. "From Earth, you'd see it travel one light-year of distance in one year. But for the astronauts on board the spaceship, it would have taken less time. Like seven weeks. So in that way, they'd be about ten months in the future. Does that make sense?"

"Sort of," Roya said, trying to wrap her head around it. "So then . . . would they be ten months younger?"

Baba nodded so enthusiastically, Roya worried for a moment about his bony neck being able to handle it. "Yes, exactly! I mean, that's the theory, anyway. No one can actually travel at the speed of light, at least not yet."

"Hmmm," Roya said, frowning. "But Grandmother isn't a spaceship. And she doesn't appear to be moving."

"That's true. There's also another theory called the Tipler cylinder, where basically a rotating cylinder of very dense material could create a wormhole that has the same effect as traveling at a great speed," Baba continued.

"Oooh. A cylinder." Roya perked up. "Maybe there's one of those inside the cabinet?"

"Well . . . probably not," Baba admitted. "Tipler's theoretical cylinder would be so enormous that scientists haven't been able to build it in the real world. Yet."

Yet had always been one of Baba's favorite words. The few times Roya had gone with him to his school, during Take Your Kid to Work Days, she'd noticed how often he used it in his lectures. Almost as often as he used it at home. But she hadn't heard him use it in a while. Maybe because *yet* had come to mean something sinister for their family. Baba himself hadn't *yet* . . . She couldn't even bring herself to think of the word.

"Before Tipler, there was a lesser-known physicist who had a similar theory." Baba's words took Roya out of her dark thoughts. "He was actually Einstein's assistant for a while. His name was Cornelius Lanczos, and his idea of a rotating cylinder could have been much smaller. Though still not small enough to fit into a cabinet, I don't think."

"Wait," Roya said. "What did you say his name was?"

"Cornelius Lanczos. He was Hungarian, I believe."

"That sounds an awful lot like 'Cornelius Lank'!" Roya said excitedly. "Stefanie said that was the name of the mechanic who helped Ivan build Grandmother as a surprise for Natasha. I remember because . . . well, Cornelius Lank is a pretty memorable name. And I wrote it down in my journal."

"Really?" Baba looked elated. "That would be an awful big coincidence if they weren't somehow the same person."

Roya nodded furiously. "You know, I bet Amin would love to talk to you about this stuff too. Do you think I can FaceTime you with him sometime? I'll make sure you're awake first." This caused her another pang as Baba's fatigue was what she thought of as a Traffic Cone Subject, a topic she usually swerved hard to avoid.

"Of course!" Baba said. "I'd be delighted to meet your new friend."

"You'll love him," Roya gushed. "He's brilliant. And get this, he *loooooves* research. I'm sure he'll have a ton of questions to ask you."

Baba chuckled. "A man after my own heart."

AFTER HER VISIT WITH BABA, Roya took a slightly different route home from her subway stop so she'd be sure to walk past Taste of Bangla, where Amin had told her he'd be all day. It was the first time she'd stepped into his family's restaurant, a small and charming place with dark wood furniture and pretty gold flourishes on the walls and counters.

"Good afternoon, Roya," Mrs. Lahiri greeted her as soon as she walked in. She was dressed in a deep purple outfit today. "Are you looking for Amin?"

Roya nodded and Mrs. Lahiri smiled warmly as she pointed out a corner table all the way in the back of the restaurant. Roya could see the back of Amin's head as he hunched over something. It was in between lunch and dinner, so the restaurant was empty except for them.

"Hi!" she said as she approached.

He looked up from the book he was reading. Roya tilted her head to read the title: *An Introduction to Theories of Time Travel.* "Find out anything?" she asked.

"I got to a chapter about parallel universes," Amin said.

"And a theory that if time travel is possible, it could create multiple versions of the same person that exist at the same time."

"Whoa," Roya said. "I learned some stuff from my dad too."

"Oh! What did he say?" Amin asked.

Roya plopped down in the seat across from him. "It's a little complicated. Probably would be easier for me to play the recording for you." She took out the recorder from her backpack, found the last file, and pressed play.

While they were listening, Mr. Lahiri walked over with a few small plates that he set in front of Roya. "A sampler for you. Kathi rolls," Mr. Lahiri said as he pointed at a dish that looked like flaky folded-up pancakes. "Aloo posto," he explained, pointing at a dish of potatoes smothered with a thick brown paste. "And chops." He pointed to neat, pocket-sized rolls of deep-fried meat. There was a variety of sauces in small cups next to each plate.

"And Amin's 'chops,'" Mr. Lahiri said as he set a plate in front of Amin. Roya was surprised to see that it contained only plain, beige chicken nuggets. Amin didn't seem to notice the food. The recording had gotten to the part about Cornelius Lanczos, and he was utterly entranced.

Roya picked up a kathi roll and bit in. It was filled with flavorful veggies and sauce that meshed perfectly with the delicate, flaky pastry surrounding it. She hungrily took another bite.

"We'll have to do more research on Cornelius Lanczos at the library," Amin said once the recording had ended.

"Agreed," Roya said.

Amin seemed to hesitate for a moment before he asked shyly, "What you said to your dad about me . . . do you really think I'm brilliant?"

"Of course," Roya said as she stuffed her face with the potatoes. They were a little spicy but in a pleasant way that made her mouth tingle. "Doesn't everybody?"

"Um, no," Amin said. "Mostly they just think I'm weird." He eyed the wide array of dishes in front of Roya before saying in a quieter voice, "Especially since I find food so overwhelming."

"Do you?" Roya asked. It was an open-ended question posed with only curiosity, no judgment. It was one of the podcast interviewing techniques she was honing.

Amin nodded. "There are just so many scents. And textures. And then to put all that in your *mouth*." He physically shuddered.

"Do the smells of the restaurant bother you, then?" Roya asked.

"Not the spices my dad uses. Maybe because I'm used to them," Amin said. "But I can only handle the smells. Not the tastes."

"Is that what you work on in food therapy? Do you try new foods?"

"Sometimes," Amin said. "Mostly we talk about food. What

it feels like. What it sounds like. If I have any emotions like fear or anxiety tied to a certain food."

"Fascinating," Roya said.

Amin snorted. "That I'm the kid of a chef and I don't eat any of the stuff he makes?" He picked up one of his chicken nuggets and bit into it. "I know that's weird."

Roya shook her head. "Nope. Like I said, it's fascinating. Obviously you feel and hear and see things that most people don't. Like you're more in tune with the world."

"That's what it feels like," Amin said. "Sometimes it makes me feel like I'm crazy."

"Not crazy. Brilliant," Roya said firmly. "Just like I told Baba. And anyway, I'd bet people thought kid Einstein or kid Cornelius was weird or crazy too."

Amin grinned. "Can I really FaceTime with your baba sometime?"

Roya nodded. "But it wouldn't be for a few days," she warned. "He needs time to recover from his treatments tomorrow."

"What sort of treatments?" Amin asked.

Roya hesitated. But then she thought about how forthcoming Amin had been about his food issues. "He's on chemo."

"Chemotherapy?" Amin asked.

"Yes."

"For cancer?"

Roya swallowed. She avoided that word at almost all costs. "Yes," she said, her voice scratchy.

"What kind of cancer?"

Roya cleared her throat before she answered, "Colon."

"Is it bad?" Amin asked.

Roya gulped a huge balloon of air. She could lie. After all, she usually didn't tell people Baba was sick at all, which was its own form of lying. But it was harder to do it outright. And even though she hadn't known Amin very long, it seemed even harder to do to him. So she just nodded.

"I'm sorry," Amin said.

Roya blinked a few times before she said, "Did you discover anything else today?"

"Yes!" Amin said, taking out his timeline paper. "Are you ready?"

Roya nodded, *so* ready to talk about anything else.

"Stefanie and I went back to the dates on the original fortune. And we realized that not only were they all in July, but . . ." Amin looked at Roya, pausing for effect. "They were all the same day of the week! A Monday!"

"And when we saw Katya . . . ," Roya said, immediately understanding what Amin was getting at.

"It was also a Monday," Amin confirmed. "So I think that's the only day of the week Grandmother opens the gate for time travel. And maybe we can only go once per Monday, which is why we weren't able to go through again."

"But next Monday, it'll be August," Roya said. "The other dates all fall in July."

Amin nodded. "I'm not sure if it'll work, but . . ."

"We have to try." Roya finished his sentence. "Do we have a plan, then?"

Amin grinned. "Stefanie has already gotten the day off."

Throwback

AMIN SPENT THE FEW DAYS before Monday in the library, and sometimes Roya joined him. But more often, she was scripting Katya's episode of the podcast. "5J: The Mystery of the Clogged Bathtub" remained half edited and unposted for now while Roya thought about how she would structure Katya's story. The first segment should probably dive into what happened on their last trip to Coney Island and end with Amin revealing his theory that they might be—cue dramatic sound effect—time-traveling. She spent part of the weekend recording lines with Amin, who took direction quite well. Roya was pleased with their progress.

Roya was also busy helping Aty out with the large construction project and, when not recording, was often being sent on errands to the hardware store. She also had to take charge entirely on the day that Aty took Baba to his chemotherapy session. They were both so preoccupied that Roya felt like she hadn't had the opportunity to sit down and tell Aty all their latest theories about Katya. Or, at least, that's what Roya kept telling herself. A couple of times, Aty mentioned in passing that she hoped Roya, Amin, and Stefanie flyering Coney Island with pictures of Katya would help, and Roya didn't go out of her way to correct her as to what they were really doing down there.

On Monday morning, Roya met Amin and Stefanie at her door, and they set off together. Roya recorded all through the subway ride, getting Amin to discuss some of what he'd learned about time travel. "I don't understand all of it," he warned, but judging from how well he could explain it, it seemed like he understood quite a bit. He was a compelling narrator. And maybe if there was a day when Baba was feeling up to it, she could get both of them to dissect the nitty-gritty of time travel for a bonus episode.

At the entrance to Deno's Park, Roya took over, narrating where they were going and what she could see. "We walk past the bright red, white, and yellow lights at the gate, and past the kiddie fire trucks and carousel. We're going through the colorful ramp that says 'Coney Island' on the walls and 'Fun, Games, Excitement, Thrills This Way.' It's a great photo op if you're ever able to come here on a quieter day, when hundreds of people wouldn't be annoyed at you for blocking their way."

From the corner of her eye, Roya saw Stefanie look over at her with a bemused smile. She had asked Stefanie for permission to record but hadn't told her about the podcast, of course. If Stefanie wondered why Roya seemed so skilled at narrating their movements, she didn't ask.

"And there she is: Grandmother," Roya continued into her recorder as they approached the cabinet. "She doesn't look like anything special. Not unless you know our story."

She turned to Amin and Stefanie. "I'm going to keep recording as we try to, uh . . . what are we calling it? Go through?"

"Disrupt the space–time continuum?" Amin suggested.

"That works," Roya said. "Ready to disrupt?" She looked over at Stefanie, whose face was set in grim determination. It was the doctor face Roya had seen the one time she'd needed stitches and Stefanie happened to be working at the ER.

"I'm ready," Stefanie said. They linked hands, Stefanie to Roya, Roya to Amin. Amin took out the two coins and put one in, then the other.

A click and then the blip. Everything went dark and silent for one nanosecond.

When the world flickered into focus around them, the weather wasn't different this time. It was still a sunny summer day, so they maybe hadn't actually traveled at all.

But something *was* different. Roya's one hand still held on to Amin's, but the other one . . . was empty. Stefanie wasn't there.

Roya searched the faces closest to her. No Stefanie or Katya.

Besides Amin, there was no one that she recognized at all. But the feeling of strangeness didn't just stem from that. There were a lot of people, dressed in regular-looking jeans and T-shirts, only many of them had a small black, blinking device clipped to their pockets, some of which were beeping. One or two people were talking into their phones. At least, Roya thought that's what they were doing. They were holding chunky black-and-silver blocks to their ears, a long, thin antenna coming out of them. Then she saw a couple of people who were definitely talking into phones . . . pay phones. Little booths with a large silver console in the middle she had only ever seen in the background of some old throwback photos Aty had posted online once.

When she looked around, she realized something else: Grandmother didn't look the same, either. Her cabinet was red and white, for one thing, not the dark wood they were used to. And her wig and clothes were different, her hair a much darker gray, and her clothes drabber colors. Only the wrinkled wax face and the twinkle in her glass eye were recognizable.

Roya turned to Amin, her expression as surprised as his. One look and she knew they were both thinking the same thing.

Stefanie wasn't here. And Katya wasn't here. But more than that: It seemed like they hadn't just traveled back a week or two this time. She was pretty certain that they weren't in the same year at all.

A Delicious Power

"EXCUSE ME, BUT WHAT YEAR is this?" Leave it to Amin to cut to the chase. He'd stopped a young teenage boy wearing baggy jeans and holding a skateboard, sporting just the tiniest wisp of a mustache above his lips.

"Hunh?" he asked

"The year? Could you tell me what year this is?"

The boy narrowed his eyes at Amin in a look Roya recognized: that of a lifelong New Yorker trying to figure out what the stranger talking to him might actually want. But then the boy must have accepted Amin's guileless expression, because he just shrugged and his posture relaxed. "Ninety-nine, man."

"Ninety-nine," Amin repeated. "1999?"

The boy tilted his head slightly as he said, "Yeah. 'Course."

Roya's brain reeled. 1999? *Nineteen* ninety-nine? She

widened her eyes at Amin, who looked equally stunned. "Did you think this would happen?"

Amin shook his head. "I thought we'd go back to two weeks ago again with Katya, but 1999 . . ." They looked at each other and said at the exact same time, "Katya's aunt!"

"Daria," Amin said. "Her name is Daria."

They turned to Grandmother. "Do you think she's already come and gone?" Roya looked around the cabinet. No one was nearby right now; no one even seemed to be looking in its direction.

"I don't know," Amin admitted. "But I think we have to wait around a while and see. Only . . ." He frowned.

"What?" Roya asked.

Amin said quietly, almost to himself, "My parents won't be happy there isn't an adult with us."

"Hmm," Roya said. "Well, Stefanie is probably still at Coney Island. Just, you know, in 2024. So if you think about it, she's sorta technically *here*."

Amin eyed her skeptically. "That's not the whole truth."

"It's a version of it," Roya said.

"I don't think there are such things as versions of the truth," Amin said. "It's usually pretty black and white."

Only it wasn't, Roya thought. One thing Aty was always saying was how the world wasn't *ever* black and white.

"Look," Roya said, deciding to take a different approach. "We'll just stay right here. Besides, once we use the machine again, we'll go back to our own time, right?"

Amin shrugged. "That's what happened last time, so hopefully. But there's no way to know for sure."

"Well, like you said, we have to at least try to wait for Daria." Roya thought for a few seconds. "How about we give her half an hour? Thirty minutes. And if she doesn't show up, then we try to go back through Grandmother."

Amin hesitated but then nodded. "Yes. I think that makes the most sense. We can't just leave now that we're here."

Roya gave what she hoped was an encouraging smile. Then the two of them stood to one side and took stock of their surroundings.

"It's not just Grandmother that's changed," Roya said, bringing her recorder back up to her mouth. "The bright and carefully painted graffiti on the walls leading up to the Wonder Wheel has been replaced by real graffiti. Most of them are large tagged names."

"I think these are from real street artists," Amin added. "Not people who've been paid by the park to paint on the walls."

"Hey! It's BunnytheBunny!" Roya said, pointing out the familiar handwriting to Amin. "He tagged inside our building too. On the stairwell between the third and fourth floors."

"Really?" Amin asked.

Roya nodded. "I'll have to show you when we get back."

As they waited, they observed the parkgoers milling about, chatting with each other and laughing, some of them munching on popcorn and cotton candy. They didn't look too different from the people Roya was used to seeing at Deno's Park, but something *felt* different. Something felt louder and more . . . present. It took Roya a minute to realize it was because no one was absorbed in a phone screen. Instead, everyone there was interacting with *each other.* There were groups of teenagers huddling together and kids running around, shrieking while their parents tried to calm them down. The line for the Wonder Wheel snaked around, longer than it had been a few minutes ago—or twenty-five years ago, if you wanted to get technical about it. Even the few solo people she could see sitting on the park benches in the distance were looking up instead of down: people-watching or bird-watching or just gazing out at the ocean. Roya narrated it all, trying to explain the experience of it as best she could.

"This is incredible," Amin chimed in, staring around in wonder. "We're in a whole different timeline. Before we existed."

"I know," Roya agreed.

"Do you think . . ." But Roya never got to hear what Amin was going to ask her. Instead, she watched his eyes widen and his mouth drop as he stared at someone and said in a reverent whisper, "Oh, wow. Oh, wow."

Roya followed his gaze. He was staring at a teenage girl, impeccably dressed in spangly hijab. There was something oddly familiar about her.

"Is that . . . ?" Roya asked.

"My mom," Amin provided. "It is. It's her. I've seen a photo of her in that outfit with my grandfather." Amin was looking at an older man, who seemed to be lecturing Mrs. Lahiri. Although, Roya supposed, she wouldn't be Mrs. Lahiri yet.

"What's your mom's first name?" she asked Amin.

"Rimi," Amin said. "And holy schneikees." Amin watched as Rimi rolled her eyes the moment the older man turned away. "I can't believe she just did that. The one time she saw me rolling my eyes at her, she took away my screen time." A slow smile crept across Amin's face at the realization that he had just caught his mom doing something she shouldn't be.

Roya and Amin locked eyes, both aware of the delicious power they suddenly held. Their parents were kids, meaning they weren't in charge here.

"I'm going to file this away for use later," Amin said.

They watched as Rimi followed her dad out of the park with her head down. But right before she left, she took a quick glance around, as if to make sure no one was looking, and then deliberately slapped the side of a garbage can.

Roya and Amin looked at each other, puzzled. As soon as

Rimi was out of sight, they both ran toward the garbage can and examined where Rimi's hand had touched the side.

"It's a note," Amin said in wonder. "She taped it on."

"What does it say?" Roya asked.

Amin hesitated for a second, but then his curiosity seemed to win out, because he carefully removed the tape and opened the note. "It's written in Bangla. It says: 'Meet me 10 p.m. on Tuesday in front of Jumi.' And it's signed with a heart." Amin looked up at Roya. "Jumi was the name of Taste of Bangla when it was my grandparents' restaurant. My dad's parents."

"Is the note . . . ?" Roya started to ask, but then got immediately distracted by a flash of bright red hair. "Look!"

It was someone, a woman, at Grandmother's cabinet. And Grandmother was moving her hands over her tarot cards.

"Could that be Daria?" Roya asked.

Amin squinted as the machine spat out a card. The woman bent down to pick it up.

Roya saw the sliver of lavender, and Amin must have seen it at the exact same time, because they both yelled out, "Daria!"

The woman had picked up the card before she turned around, a look of curiosity on her face at the sound of her name. And then she was gone.

16

A Reunion

ROYA AND AMIN STARED AT where Daria had been, their mouths hanging open. It was the second time they'd seen someone vanish from that exact spot, but that didn't diminish its awe factor.

"Now what do we do?" Roya asked Amin.

Amin shook his head. "I'm not sure." He checked his watch. "We're almost at the end of our half-hour limit, though."

Roya nodded. "Stefanie will worry."

"And our parents," Amin added. Roya didn't bother telling him that their parents technically didn't know they'd disappeared from Stefanie's supervision.

"Let's just look one more time for clues as to where Daria went," Roya suggested.

Amin hesitated for a moment, grappling between his senses of responsibility and curiosity, before nodding. "Okay." The two took a quick turn around the three-quarters of Grandmother's cabinet that was facing out, even ducking their heads to try to get a glimpse of the back where it was plugged in and pressed up against the other machines surrounding it. They checked the slot to make sure another fortune hadn't come out along with the one Daria took with her . . . wherever she was. But nothing, aside from the disappearing Petrov, seemed out of the ordinary.

They looked at each other and shrugged helplessly: *They'd tried.* Amin took out two coins from his pocket.

He clinked one in. Just as he was about to drop the second, a shadow appeared on the ground in front of their feet.

Maybe it was the way the shadow appeared: suddenly, as if someone had just materialized on the spot. Or maybe it was the shape of the shadow itself, a familiarity about it. Either way, it made Roya turn around. She gasped and put a hand on Amin's arm to stop him from inserting the second coin.

He turned around too.

"Katya." Roya said her name quietly this time, almost a whisper. After all, she didn't need to shout to be heard; Katya was right there in front of her, clutching her lavender paper.

The blond woman looked up and blinked. "Roya?" she asked. "So it *was* you I just saw."

Roya nodded and swallowed hard. "Well, not *just*," she

corrected Katya. "We've been looking for you. Stefanie's been so worried."

Katya blinked. "Isn't she at work? I only left the apartment half an hour ago."

"Actually," Roya said, "it's been two weeks."

"Or really, twenty-five years," Amin chimed in. "And two weeks."

Katya looked at Amin. "I just saw you too. With her." She pointed at Roya. "And wait. What did you say?"

"Let's find a bench," Roya suggested. "I think you're going to need to sit down for this."

"TIME TRAVEL," KATYA SAID, LOOKING down at the lavender paper. "Now it all makes sense." They had sat down at one of the picnic tables outside the Nathan's on the boardwalk.

"What's written on there?" Amin asked curiously.

"It says: 'Take stock in your knowledge. Make your own fortune,'" Katya read.

"What does that mean?" Roya asked.

"I think . . . ," Katya started slowly, like she was piecing it together herself as she explained. "I think if we're really in the past, then it means I should be able to use my knowledge of what companies do well in the future to invest in them now.

For example, knowing Apple is going to invent the iPhone." She stared off into space for a moment before turning her attention back to Roya and Amin. "Do you know what year we're in?"

"1999," Roya offered.

"We saw Daria," Amin added.

Katya gasped. "You did?"

Roya nodded. "Right before you turned up. Maybe she went back to . . ." She looked at Amin, who had a better grasp of the exact timeline.

"1974? Your grandmother Annika?" Amin said, and then started nodding. "That would make sense. If each Petrov goes back to the previous one's time, invests in the stocks they know will do well . . ."

"The money," Katya said softly. "I was hoping I could somehow get it without disappearing, but I guess that's not possible." She shook her head. "I even brought my phone with me." She reached into her pocket and took out a familiar-looking smartphone with a dark screen. "I sent Stefanie a pin with my location. Thought if I kept my GPS on . . ."

"But that technology would be useless here. In this time," Amin concluded.

"Right," Katya said, staring at the device. "Stefanie must be so angry. She told me not to go, that any precautions I took would be no match for Grandmother."

"She's not angry," Roya said. "She's devastated. You have to come back with us, Katya. Grandmother told us we have one chance to save you, and I think this is it."

"Yes, of course," Katya said quietly, looking at the lavender paper wistfully. "Guess this money isn't going to help us start a family if I'm not there to start a family with." She sighed, then straightened her shoulders and folded the paper up resolutely, stuffing it in her pocket next to her phone. "Okay, so how do we get back?"

"When we did it before, it was through Grandmother. Same as how you got here," Roya explained.

"Excuse me, but . . . Katya?" They looked up to see a middle-aged woman with red hair, the kind of vibrant color that could only come out of a box, and a smear of magenta lipstick. There was something familiar about her, and she seemed to be squinting at the features of Katya's face, as if she was trying to place them too.

"Yes?" Katya said.

"Oh, but you've grown up so beautifully," the woman said, her eyes now filling with tears.

Katya's jaw dropped. "Aunt Daria?"

The woman nodded frantically. "You remember me?"

"Yes, of course." Katya sprang up and launched herself into the woman's arms, giving Roya and Amin time to examine the older woman's face better. It was more lined, and the cheeks a bit fuller, but it was definitely the aged-up face of the woman they'd just seen in front of Grandmother. Roya and Amin looked at each other in wonder.

"Oh, my Katy bug," Daria was saying into Katya's shoulder. "We have so much to talk about."

"Katy bug," Katya said. "I remember you calling me that!"

"Well, you were considerably smaller. And more bug-like," Daria said with a laugh. She pulled away to look at Katya's face and caught a glimpse of Roya and Amin staring at them. She eyed them curiously. "And who are you two?"

"I'm Roya and this is Amin," Roya said. "We're . . . well, we're from Katya's time. Her original time."

Daria's jaw dropped. "Katya, you were able to bring other people with you?"

"No, they came on their own," Katya said. "And they left later than I did." She looked to the kids for clarification. "Right?"

Amin nodded. "Two weeks later. But we ended up here."

Daria looked surprised. "I thought this was strictly a Petrov family talent. Are you part of the family too?"

Roya shook her head. "We're not Petrovs. Just friends of theirs. Well, friends of Katya and Stefanie."

"Stefanie?" Daria asked.

"My wife," Katya explained.

Daria smiled. "Congratulations," she said as she patted Katya's hand. But she looked sad too, and Roya realized that she must know, quite acutely, what it was like to leave people behind.

"So you've been here since 1974," Amin said slowly to Daria. "Is that right?"

Daria nodded. "Yes, exactly. And now that my younger self has already traveled today, the barrier has lifted. I've been waiting twenty-five years to come here and tell the next traveler everything I know about how this all works. I didn't know who it would be since I never had a daughter, but"—she looked fondly at Katya—"I was hoping I'd see you again."

Roya and Amin stared at each other, their excitement building. It sounded like they were finally about to get an explanation.

"Wait!" Roya said. "Before you start, do you mind if I record you?" She waved her pocket recorder. "It's for a podcast."

"A what?" Daria asked at the same time that Katya looked at Roya and asked, "You have a podcast?"

"Just a practice one," Roya lied hastily.

Katya smiled again and said, "Of course you do." She turned back to Daria. "It's sort of what they call radio shows in the future."

"Ah," Daria said, and then turned to Roya with a warm smile of her own. "Then by all means, record away. Though I think you might want to wait for them too."

Daria looked off into the distance and waved her hands, as if she was signaling for someone. And sure enough, someone came. Two someones, actually. Two older ladies with white hair, one more hunched and wrinkled than the other, both with the twinkly blue eyes that Daria and Katya shared too.

"Mama," Daria said, looking at the younger of the two women. "And Babushka. Meet your granddaughter and great-granddaughter, Katya."

17
The Traveling Petrovs

ANNIKA, WHICH ROYA REMEMBERED WAS the name of Katya's grandmother, immediately went over and cradled Katya's face between her hands. "Hello, baby girl," she said before giving her a huge hug.

From the other side, Polina, Katya's great-grandmother, leaned in and put her arms around the two of them. She looked about a hundred years old, but her gravelly voice sparked with energy as she said, "Hello, darling. We've been waiting for you."

"You have?" Katya asked, the tears in her eyes making them sparkle as bright blue as the Atlantic Ocean.

Daria nodded as Annika said, "Couldn't wait to see you."

"And we're also here to tell you the rules," Polina added.

"Rules?" Katya asked.

"Ooh, can I do it?" Daria asked, suddenly sounding like a

little kid. After Annika and Polina nodded, she turned to Roya and Amin to explain. "I've been waiting twenty-five years to finally be the one who has the answers, you know?" She winked before turning back to Katya. "Okay, so rule number one, you can't have any contact with our family. Not the other version of our family that exists, anyway. We call them the Original Petrovs. So like, right now, in 1999, Original Katya would be four. But you can't go see yourself then. Or your mom or me or anybody. If you try, you'll meet up with a barrier."

"A barrier?" Katya asked. "Like a physical barrier?" She, Roya, and Amin were all raptly listening to Daria as Annika and Polina took seats at the picnic table too.

"Yup. They're invisible," Daria said. "But they'll feel physical. You can't move past them. Our whole building, for example, is off-limits. And so is most of the surrounding area. Or any-place where the Original Petrovs might be at a given moment."

"Then how come you can talk to Katya?" Roya asked.

"Ah," Daria said. "Well, that's the interesting part. This new version of us, the Traveling Petrovs, seems to exist in a different timeline. And since Katya and I are both travelers, we can intersect and meet. But I couldn't get into Deno's until my younger self had left."

"Parallel universes," Amin mouthed to Roya.

Katya looked at her family. "So you all came here for me?"

"Of course!" Daria said. "Someone's gotta show you the ropes. Better than leaving you a manual, right?"

She winked and Katya giggled in a way that made her sound much younger. She then threw herself into her aunt's arms again. "I missed you, Aunt Daria."

"I missed you too, kiddo," Daria said, resting her chin atop Katya's shoulder. "It's really good to see you. Even if that's selfish of me to say."

"So what happens now?" Katya asked. "Do the three of you live together?"

"Mama and Babushka do," Daria said. "I live in the same building. Two floors down."

"But it's not *our* building, is it?" Roya asked, indicating herself, Amin, and Katya.

Daria looked quizzically at her. "The one on Ocean Parkway?" Roya nodded, and Daria shook her head. "No. Like I said, that whole building is one giant barrier." She then looked more closely at Roya and Amin. "So tell us more about yourselves, then. You also live in the Queen?"

"I just moved in a month ago," Amin said quietly.

"And I've been there my whole life," Roya said. "My mom is the super."

"Ah," Polina said, looking wistful. "How is she? The Queen, I mean?"

"Good," Roya responded. "Probably has the same elevators as when you were there."

"Really?" Polina asked.

"Really," Roya responded, and mimed pulling open the elevator door. Polina laughed.

"How come you two can travel, then?" Annika asked. "In all this time, I've never heard of anyone but the Petrovs coming through. We always assumed it was because Grandmother was a Petrov too." She pointed at the machine. "Or at least made in the likeness of one."

"We're not really sure, but . . ." Roya turned to Amin, who suddenly seemed to look a little queasy. "You okay?" Roya asked him.

He blinked a few times before turning to Roya. "Yes," he said. "Sorry, we're so close to the smells of the food here." He pointed vaguely at everyone tucking into their lunches right around them. "They're just . . . a lot."

"We can move," Roya said, and immediately got up, putting her hand over her eyes to look out toward the ocean. "How about that bench right there?"

The four women got up without protest and started to walk over. "You were saying," Daria asked before they'd even reached the bench. "About why you can travel?"

Amin took deep breaths of the salty air and started looking much calmer. He cleared his throat before he spoke. "We're not exactly sure except that Grandmother gave us a fortune, and I think it gave us permission to travel too. Only we can go back and forth."

Daria's, Annika's, and Polina's eyes all widened. "Back and forth?" Polina repeated. "As in back to your own time?"

Roya nodded. "Yes, but only on Mondays, it seems. First, we traveled back to two weeks ago, to the day that Katya disappeared. And now to here, 1999."

"Which means," Amin said, "I'm pretty sure if we leave next Monday, we'd go back another twenty-five years, to when you first disappeared." He turned to Annika, and Roya suddenly understood something.

"Grandmother's fortune to us said 'You have one chance to save her,'" she stated, and Amin nodded. "And if what you're thinking is true, then we might never go back to a time where we'd see Katya again. Which means our one chance . . ."

"Might be right here and now," Amin said.

Roya turned to Katya. "You have to try to come back with us. To Stefanie."

Katya blinked and looked around at Daria, Annika, and Polina. The impact of what Roya had said seemed to hit her slowly at first, but then her face crumpled. This was family she had just found, family she hadn't known she would ever see again. They blinked back at her, the same look of shock and sadness reflected in their eyes. For a moment, no one spoke.

Until it was Polina who put one soft, wrinkled hand on top of her great-granddaughter's. "Katyonok, we don't want to lose you now. But if any of us had the chance to go back and see our children grow up, we would take it in a heartbeat. Go." Annika and Daria nodded behind her.

"I don't have children yet," Katya said, looking down at the lavender paper. "But I'm supposed to. This money was supposed to help us."

"Then can you think of some companies to invest in?" Daria asked. "That will do well in the future? We can try to do it without you."

Katya looked bewildered, but she put a hand on her pocket, where the rectangular bulk of her smartphone was recognizable. "Do you have a pen?" she asked. Polina procured one and a slip of paper from her purse, and Roya watched as Katya quickly scribbled down the names of some tech companies.

"You sure it'll work?" Katya asked as she handed the slip of paper to Daria. "If I'm not here?"

"We're not sure about much, but we can certainly try," Polina said.

"Maybe that's why the years on the original fortune stopped at 2024," Annika added wisely. "It was always supposed to end with you."

"Right," Katya said. "Yes." She reached over and hugged them, the four women huddling together for a brief moment. Polina was the first one to pull away. "Go," she said again, placing a hand on Katya's face.

Katya nodded and turned to Roya, tears sparkling in her eyes. "Okay. I shouldn't keep Stefanie waiting any longer."

The six of them marched up to Grandmother together, Roya and Amin leading the way while the four Petrov women clasped hands behind them, walking as one unit for the first and probably last time.

When they got to Grandmother's Predictions, Katya looked at her aunt, grandmother, and great-grandmother. "Now I know what they mean by love at first sight," she said, laughing a little through her tears.

Annika placed her hand on Katya's face. "We love you too. We're so happy we got to see you, even if it was only for this little bit of time."

"You will break the curse, Katyonok," Polina said. "And no more Petrovs will have to make the sacrifices we did."

Katya embraced them all one last time, and then turned to Roya and Amin. "Okay. Ready."

Roya took her hand and Amin took Roya's. She felt a sense of déjà vu of something that had happened both an hour ago and twenty-five years in the future.

She was worried because she couldn't help remembering her empty hand where Stefanie's was supposed to be. Stefanie hadn't been able to travel with Roya and Amin. But maybe Katya was different. After all, she had already traveled before. And what Annika had said about the dates stopping after 2024— that *must* be the reason. Katya had given the Traveling Petrovs enough information to replenish the family fortune one last time. But Katya herself was meant to go back with Roya and Amin, and the time-traveling would stop with her.

Roya closed her eyes and sent out another gratitude manifestation. "Thank you, universe, for letting Katya come back with us."

She kept her eyes closed as she heard the clink of one of Amin's coins. Then the second clink.

She could sense the blip of darkness even through her closed eyelids. And she could sense something else, even before she opened her eyes.

Her left hand was empty. Katya had not made it through.

18
Pieces of the Puzzle

"THANK HEAVENS YOU TWO ARE safe!" They hadn't even turned around before someone was enveloping them in a huge bear hug, the faint scent of lavender soap instantly familiar to Roya. "You were gone for so much longer this time."

"We're okay," Roya said into Stefanie's elbow, even though her heart was sinking at the realization that they'd failed in their mission.

Stefanie looked them both up and down, the cool gaze of a medical professional briefly overtaking the panic in her eyes.

"Excuse me, are you using that?" A woman in her early twenties was standing behind them, holding the hand of a man around the same age. She was indicating Grandmother, which the three of them were currently blocking.

Stefanie glanced at Amin and Roya questioningly and

waited for them to shake their heads no before she answered the woman. "No. Sorry about that." The three of them moved to the side.

"What happened?" Stefanie asked. "Why were you gone for so long?"

"How long?" Amin asked.

Stefanie checked her watch. "Over an hour."

Amin turned to Roya. "So that means the time there is running parallel, not faster or slower. We were there for about an hour too, right?"

Roya nodded. "I think so."

"Did you see Katya again?" Stefanie asked.

"Yes. We talked to her," Roya said, and watched Stefanie's eyes light up. "We also saw Daria."

"What?" Stefanie asked. "Katya's aunt?"

Roya nodded. "And also her grandmother. And great-grandmother. Amin was right. It *is* time travel. But this time we traveled back further. To 1999."

Stefanie sucked in a breath. "What?!"

"Let's find a bench," Roya said for the second time that same day, but not, she realized, that same century.

THEY ENDED UP ON THE same ocean-view bench they'd shared with Katya and her family as they told their story. Stefanie listened intently.

"1999," she repeated. "All of them there. I can hardly believe it. And Katya tried to come back with you?"

Roya nodded fervently. "She wanted to very much. But for some reason, she couldn't."

Stefanie worried her lip. "Just like I couldn't. I wonder why you two can go through."

"Me too," Amin interjected enthusiastically. "The other Traveling Petrovs had never heard of someone outside the family going through. And they didn't know of anyone going back and forth. I don't know if Grandmother *gave* us that ability . . . or if she gave us that fortune because we already *had* the ability . . . but one thing is clear: it's up to us to save Katya."

"But what if this was our one shot to do it?" Roya said. "And we blew it?"

"I don't know. But maybe we can talk to your dad now?" Amin said.

Roya nodded. "If he's feeling up to it." She averted her eyes from Stefanie's. She and Katya were probably the only two tenants in the building who knew about Baba's illness, aside from Amin now, but she still tried to never bring it up.

Stefanie seemed too distracted to ask after him anyhow. "So we need to come back here next Monday, don't we?" She looked up at the two kids in a way that grown-ups, even grown-ups as kind and interested as Stefanie, hardly ever did. It was because she actually *needed* them; they seemed to be the only ones who could help her. "So you can find a way to bring Katya back."

Roya and Amin took one look at each other before they both answered confidently, "Yes."

"We'll get her back home, Stefanie," Roya added. "Even if we have to travel a thousand years to do it."

The Unread Note

"I HAVE A PROBLEM." AMIN was at Roya's door, frowning.

"Me too," Roya said.

"Oh no," Amin said, frowning more deeply. "What is it?"

Roya was taken aback by Amin's serious face. "My recorder didn't pick up a thing when we went to the past. Just a whole hour of glitchy beeps. So I don't have anything for the podcast."

"I think my problem might be much bigger than that," Amin said as he opened his hand to show a folded-up piece of paper.

Roya peered closer. "Is that your mom's note? From 1999?"

Amin nodded. "In all the excitement, I forgot I'd stashed it in my pocket. I accidentally brought it back with me. It was meant for my dad and, well, he never got it."

"So what does that mean?" Roya asked.

Amin shook his head. "I don't know exactly what it changed, but things are different between them. Like colder somehow.

And guess what? My mom doesn't work front-of-house at our restaurant anymore."

Roya's eyes widened. "Wow. Really? How could a missing note affect that?"

"Have you ever heard of something called the butterfly effect?"

Roya thought for a moment. "I don't think so."

"It's this theory that everything is connected—sometimes in unknowable ways—like the way a butterfly flapping its wings in Brazil could cause a tornado halfway around the world," Amin explained. "Well, that could apply to time travel. Meaning if you change one tiny thing in the past, it could have unexpected consequences in the future. Like, maybe, you removed a note you weren't supposed to in 1999." Amin stared down at the seemingly innocent piece of paper in his hand. "I haven't figured out exactly how to ask my parents about this yet, but it clearly changed *some*thing. And if it had changed enough, then it's possible the consequences could have been huge. Like maybe they'd have never gotten married. And I would've never been born."

"Whoa," Roya said, a little stunned.

"I know," Amin said.

"Well . . . I'm visiting my dad in a few hours. I think he'd be a good person to ask about this."

Amin's face brightened. "Good idea."

"We usually try to limit in-person visitors because of germs, but I can FaceTime you when I get there."

"Yes, please," Amin said.

FOR THE FIRST TIME IN a long time, Roya was visibly excited to go visit Baba. Aty immediately noticed her change in mood, remarking, "It's nice that you're volunteering to go."

It was because today, Roya had a purpose, a purpose beyond seeing how frail her dad had gotten. She only hoped he was feeling well enough to talk.

He was in the living room when she arrived, and he was awake, two excellent signs. She asked him whether it would be okay to FaceTime Amin. "Is this your friend interested in time travel?" Baba asked.

Roya nodded. "Well, now we're both interested in time travel. But I'll tell you the story when we're both here."

Amin answered his dad's tablet right away.

"Hello, Mr. Alborzi," he said to Roya's dad.

"Hello, Amin," Baba replied. He didn't say *Call me Payman.* Unlike Aty, Baba had a more traditional view of how kids, including his own, should address him. "It's nice to finally meet you. Roya's told me a lot about you. So, what's going on?"

Amin nodded toward Roya. She had told him that she wanted to be the one to break the big news. "We did it, Baba!" she blurted out. "We really time-traveled again. And this time we went back *years*."

"Years?" Baba asked.

Roya nodded. "To 1999."

"Oh my," Baba said, and Roya could swear she saw some color in his hollow cheeks. "Are you sure?"

Amin spoke up. "We asked someone the year. And then we saw Daria, Katya's aunt—"

"And then we saw Katya herself again."

"As a kid?" Baba asked.

Roya shook her head. "No, as an adult. She had just gone through. And then the older version of Daria, her grandmother, and her great-grandmother showed up too."

Baba whistled. "Incredible."

Roya grinned. "It really happened! So I think Cornelius Lank must've been—"

"Cornelius Lanczos." Baba's eyes crinkled and glowed in a way Roya hadn't seen in a long time. "Well, I'll be," he said as he chuckled. "I'll be." He looked off into the distance for a second, his gaze filled with wonder.

"The only problem is," Roya continued, "when we tried to bring Katya back with us, she couldn't go through."

"And we're trying to figure out why," Amin said. "Maybe it's something to do with our masses? We're smaller?"

"Hmmm. That's an interesting thought. Mass is a part of the equation when it comes to theoretical time travel. But then again . . . well, this isn't quite theoretical, is it?" Baba's face shone with excitement.

Both Roya and Amin shook their heads.

"Tell me more," Baba said. "What did it feel like exactly? What did you do?"

So Roya told him about holding Stefanie's hand but losing her once the blip happened. She told him about the lack of smartphones, asking the year, and seeing Original Daria and then Katya—how Katya's phone didn't work there, either. She explained the three Traveling Petrov women and some of the rules they had laid out: how they couldn't interfere with themselves or their family in their original timeline but how the travelers could be together. And then, finally, she told him about coming through without Katya. "And there's one more thing," Roya said, and she nodded at Amin through the screen, giving him the go-ahead to share what else had happened in 1999.

"I saw my mom. A younger version of my mom. And she was leaving a note for my dad," Amin said. "I accidentally took the note back with me, which means the teen version of my dad never got it. And now some things in the present have changed. I think it has something to do with the butterfly effect."

"I see," Baba said. "Yes. That is a popular theory of time travel. Are these big changes or small changes?"

"Sort of small," Amin said. "My mom doesn't work. But also . . . I don't know. She doesn't seem as happy? I can't totally explain it. There's just a shift in mood in my house that I can feel more than see. But they still got together, obviously, since I exist. And they still *are* together."

Baba stayed quiet for a moment, thinking. "And the Petrovs talked to you about their barriers?"

Roya and Amin nodded.

"I wonder if that means there are other protections in place. That maybe there are some larger, immutable things that can't be changed, even if some smaller things can," Baba said slowly. "Essentials."

"Maybe," Amin said, though he was still frowning. "When we go next Monday . . ." He paused.

"Yes?" Baba encouraged.

"Well, I think we'll probably go back to a different year. 1974," Amin said. "When Annika traveled. But I'm also worried."

"About what?" Roya asked.

"What if we disrupt something again," Amin blurted out.

"Only this time, it's something bigger. Something that affects our families more, or even ourselves."

"But Grandmother told us we have one shot to save Katya," Roya argued. "And if we haven't already missed it, doesn't that mean we're *supposed* to go back?"

"Maybe," Amin said again, still sounding unconvinced.

"Besides," Roya said confidently. "What about the big, immutable things, like my baba just said?"

"Well," Baba said gently, "that's only a theory, Roya."

"But an educated one," Roya said.

"Hmmm," Baba said as he leaned back in his chair. Roya was a bit surprised by Baba's lack of concern about the possible dangers of her travels. After all, Baba had never been like Aty when it came to giving Roya so much freedom. But Roya attributed it to a combination of his scientific curiosity and his physical exhaustion.

"Could you show me a picture of the fortune-telling machine?" Baba asked.

"Of course," Roya said, and she Googled it on his phone to show him the cabinet. She even found a picture of what it used to look like. "That was Grandmother in 1999. And this is her now."

"The machine was restored after Hurricane Sandy in 2012," Amin offered, which was new information he must've come across in his research.

"Looks much smaller than any theoretical time-travel machine I've ever read about," Baba said. "Even Lanczos's idea of a rotating cylinder was never that small. But then again . . ."

"The world is full of mysteries?" Roya offered up one of her father's own favorite platitudes.

Baba grinned at his daughter. "Exactly, azizam."

Plot Twist

"THAT'S A PICTURE OF POLINA by the Wonder Wheel! Look!" Amin pointed at a large, blurry circle in the background of the black-and-white photo.

Stefanie and Roya peered closer at it. "You're right," Stefanie said. "Let's see if this has a date." She slid the old photo out of the four corner tabs that were keeping it inside the leather-bound album. When she flipped it over, it said on the back, in pencil: *1948*.

"A year before she disappeared," Amin said out loud, and then flipped the photo back over to study the smiling blond woman sitting on the beach in a one-piece bathing suit. She had a resemblance to the Polina that they had seen but was, of course, much younger.

"Wait! How could I have not thought of this before?" Roya said, looking closer at the picture. "The Wonder Wheel is a sort of rotating cylinder. A bigger one than could fit inside the cabinet."

Amin's eyes widened. "And Grandmother is called the Guardian of the Wheel. The owners of the park were instructed to never separate them."

"So that could have something to do with how Cornelius got the time travel to work," Roya finished, looking back at the picture of Polina. "And if our theory is correct, Polina would've gone back to 1924."

Amin nodded. "So when we see her on Monday, she'll be about fifty years older than this."

"Right," Stefanie said. "About that . . ." She closed the album and cleared her throat. "I've thought a lot about this, and, honestly, we need to tell your parents everything. Before we go again." She looked over at Amin, whose face had filled with concern. "I'm sorry, Amin. But who knows exactly what we're playing with here? I need them to be aware of what's going on before they agree to send you on another trip with me."

"Okay," Amin said shakily. "I'll . . . try to explain."

Stefanie nodded. "And if you need me to be there when you do, I'm happy to back you up." She turned to Roya with a smile. "And I assume you've already told Aty everything?"

A small acidic wave washed across Roya's stomach as she hesitated. "Er . . ."

"You haven't?" Stefanie looked surprised.

"I, um, told Baba," Roya said. "Aty's been busy." Which was the truth. But not the whole truth. Roya didn't know exactly why she was hesitant to confide in Aty, only that it had felt better to keep parts of the story to herself. And it was easy to convince herself that it was the right thing to do too. Aty wanted her to be independent, right? Well, she was independently investigating this great mystery.

"You have to tell Aty too," Stefanie said gently. "Okay?"

Roya hesitated one more time, then nodded. "Of course."

ROYA WAITED UNTIL A LITTLE after 9:00 p.m., the only time Aty unwound a little because it was less likely a tenant would text or knock with a problem. Aty's version of unwinding was sitting in the leather armchair with a small glass of tea and either doodling in her sketchbook or reading a graphic novel.

Roya looked at the cover of the new book Aty had just picked up from the library. The illustration on the front showed the silhouette of a large manor house with a bolt of lightning behind it, a man with a bowler hat and a large mustache standing in front.

Definitely a mystery.

Maybe that's my in, Roya thought. *Aty loves both mysteries and myths, and here's a real-life one.*

"Did I tell you," Roya began as she sat down on the edge of the love seat next to the armchair, "that we saw Katya?"

Aty immediately put her book down. "What?" she said, startled. "She's back?"

"Well, um . . . in a way." After all, Katya *was* back—just back in time as opposed to back in their building. Roya cleared her throat. "Amin and I saw her last week," Roya began. "And then, we saw her again on Monday."

Aty remained quiet, brown eyes staring into Roya's exact-same-shade-of-brown. She was giving Roya the space to recount the story in her own way. But somehow it felt like too much space; like Roya was in a galaxy and asked to pick a star, any star.

Roya fiddled with a button on the love seat's slipcover as she spoke, blurting the story out quickly. "So apparently Grandmother is, like, some sort of time-travel machine. The first time Amin and I traveled, we only went back two weeks, to the day Katya disappeared. But the second time, we went back twenty-five years. We saw Katya again but also her grand-mother, great-grandmother, and aunt. Two versions of her aunt, actually: a young one and an older one."

Aty blinked at her. "I don't understand, Roya jaan. Slow down and tell me what you mean."

"We don't understand either exactly. Amin and I talked about it with Baba today, and we think the time travel has something to do with the Wonder Wheel itself. This scientist named Cornelius—"

"Hold on. You've spent the past week *time-traveling*. And you're telling me this . . . now?" Aty turned her signature X-ray stare on her daughter. Roya had been feeling uneasy about keeping all this from her mom, but she had an excuse ready for her—the same one she'd been telling herself.

"Well, we've been trying to figure it all out ourselves," Roya said. "And besides, you've been busy. As usual."

Aty paused before asking, "So then is Katya back? Here?"

Roya shook her head. "We tried to bring her back with us, but for some reason, she couldn't travel back. Stefanie couldn't come through with us either. It seems like it's just Amin and I who can go back and forth, but the portal only seems to be open on Mondays. So next Monday, we're going to try again."

"You're going," Aty asked slowly, "to try to time-travel again?"

"Yes. So that we can figure out how to bring Katya back," Roya said.

"So, as of now, Katya is stuck? In the past?" Aty asked.

Roya nodded. "It seems like it."

"And how do you know that you and Amin won't get stuck too?" Aty asked.

"Well . . . we haven't before." It was a flimsy answer, but true.

Aty put down her glass of tea, which was still only half drunk. "I'm sorry to say this, Roya, but no."

Roya blinked at her mother. "No, what?"

Aty shook her head. "No, you can't go. Sorry." She got up and took the glass of tea into the kitchen, dumping the remainder of the liquid out in the sink and then turning on the water to wash the glass.

Aty stared at her mother's back. Everything about this was out of character, starting with not finishing her tea and ending with that strange, resolute *no.*

"But, Aty. We have to. We're the *only* ones who can do this."

Aty turned off the water but stood facing the wall for one moment, then two. She was bracing herself against the sink, Roya realized, and when she finally spoke, Roya hardly recognized the voice that was coming out of her mother's mouth: it sounded so fragile, on the verge of breaking, even.

"I'm sorry, Roya. I want Katya back too. But not at the risk of losing you. I . . . can't." She still hadn't turned around.

"Aty, we're completely fine," Roya said. "Amin knows how it works."

"Amin is a kid," Aty said, turning to face her daughter at last. "You're a kid too." The words felt like an unexpected thundershower in the middle of July, like a fluffy white cloud had suddenly turned deep gray and burst open without warning.

That's how Aty's face looked too, twisted in a strange grimace of worry and sadness and, maybe, even a little bit of anger. "I can't believe your father didn't tell me any of this."

"Don't blame him," Roya said immediately. She still remembered the fights her parents used to have, particularly about her, before the divorce. After Baba moved out, they had been on much friendlier terms—especially once he got sick and Aty jumped in to take care of him. Roya didn't want any of that to change back now.

"Okay," Aty said, her voice brittle as a ceramic plate. "But I'm sorry. I have too much to worry about right now. Keeping up with the tenants alongside everything going on with your father. I can't be worrying about you *time-traveling* too. I just can't." With that, she placed her glass upside down on the drying rack and brushed past Roya to walk into her bedroom, closing the door behind her.

Roya stared at the door, stunned. She hadn't heard many nos from Aty in her life to start off with. But a no like that, a definitive no? She rubbed her hands along the wooden arm of the couch, dumbfounded. For the first time in a long time, she didn't know what to say. This was a twist she had never seen coming.

21

A Slippery Snake

ATY AND ROYA BARELY SPOKE the rest of the evening except to bid each other good night. Roya hardly slept, tossing and turning in her bed for hours. But then finally, just before dawn was about to break outside her window, a thought came into her head: there was no way Mr. and Mrs. Lahiri would say yes where Aty had said no. And somehow, that made her feel a little better. She finally fell into an uneasy sleep that was punctuated by dreams of Grandmother, only with her waxen face looking remarkably similar to Aty's grimacing one.

When Roya woke up, she felt groggy and discombobulated, almost like she hadn't slept at all. She opened her front door to take out the garbage and nearly bumped into Amin's grinning face and outstretched hand, poised as if he was about to knock. "You'll never guess what!" he said.

Roya's heart was already sinking because she *could* actually guess. "What?"

"My parents said yes! They talked to Stefanie and said it was okay as long as she was there with us. Well, as far as she could go. And as long as we didn't stay in the past without her for more than an hour." He grinned a huge grin.

"Oh." Roya's voice sounded as small as her hopes felt right now. "Did they believe you? About the time travel?"

"Well, not at first. But then I showed them the note. And told them how I accidentally took it. They were shocked. But also, my mom finally believed that my dad hadn't just stood her up all those years ago." Amin put on his dad's deeper voice to say, " 'Why you needed our son to time-travel to believe me in the first place is beyond me.' And I thought maybe they were going to argue, but then they started hugging instead."

Amin looked incandescently happy, almost the exact opposite of how Roya felt. "I think their good mood helped them say yes. But also, I think they're just happy I'm making friends and hanging out with someone my own age. Maybe that overrides how they feel about their only child being in mortal peril." He chuckled and Roya immediately felt guilty; the garden snake of envy was back and she was feeling its venom course through her veins.

"Well, that's great, Amin," she said, trying to keep her voice steady. "But I can't go. Aty said no." She brushed past Amin with the garbage bag in her hand, and had made it to the trash chute when she heard Amin's voice behind her.

"But your dad said yes. Didn't he?" he asked.

Roya closed her eyes. Everything felt too raw for Amin to say it so matter-of-factly. "Yeah," she said as she put the bag in the chute and heard it drop into the dumpster in the basement. She fixed her expression into one of nonchalance before she turned around to Amin again. She even shrugged for good measure. "But he's not really the one in charge. So."

"But I'm not even sure I can go without you," Amin said. "Like logistically. Maybe it only works if we travel together."

"I'm sorry," Roya said, swallowing and thinking of the two kids holding hands that Aty had seen in the coffee grounds. "Maybe I can, I don't know, come to the library with you the rest of the week or something. Still help out." Though the thought of doing that and sitting out the adventure part sounded brutal.

She walked past Amin now and to her door. "Sorry again," she said, and then, before her voice could betray her true emotions, she opened her door, slipped inside, and swung it shut. Then she went in search of her feelings journal—for once intending to use it for its original purpose.

ON THURSDAY, BUMBLEBEE AND BEAR in 6D were going to camp . . . again. Aty had assigned Roya some menial task . . . again. She was supposed to go to the hardware store to pick up an extra can of paint for the new apartments on the sixth floor. And she was furious. Never had her anger-red journal deserved its color more.

"Roya Alborzi, your intrepid podcast host, has been felled by that greatest of all adversaries," she recorded in her bedroom after returning from the hardware store, "the parental ban." It was funny, or it would have been if it didn't feel so arbitrary that her mom would do this *now,* when it mattered most.

What was she supposed to do now? Go back to reporting on how many times 6K did laundry or 5J clogged up their tub?

She was bored. But at the same time, when Amin asked her to go to the library, she found herself making an excuse. It was just too painful, that all she could do at this point was be a researcher instead of the investigator, the one leading the charge. Amin tried to tell her how interesting it was that "the Traveling Petrovs" was also the name of Natasha's circus troupe from the early 1900s, but all Roya could do was grunt a half-hearted "Cool. But, um, I need to go help Aty."

Aty and Roya weren't really speaking to each other, though neither one acknowledged it. Aty would ask Roya to do things around the building, and she'd do them. But there was no fortune-telling via Hafez, or drinking tea together in the living room, Aty reading and sketching while Roya put on her headphones and fiddled with editing the podcast.

Roya now hid away in her room, mostly staring at the ceiling. She thought about Katya, and Daria, and Annika, and Polina. She thought about what the Traveling Petrovs must be doing now. Where did they live? Had Katya officially moved in with her newfound family? And then she wondered if Katya would live the rest of her life somewhere out of reach. Maybe, eventually, with someone else. And she felt sad for Stefanie and the wedding she had gotten to witness, the very first wedding she'd ever been invited to. The flower crowns in both Stefanie's and Katya's hair had seemed so magical on that dance floor in the Old Stone House at the edge of the Fifth Street playground. Katya and Stefanie had even somehow bribed a park attendant to turn on the sprinklers after the wedding, so they all ran through them on the warm August night, giggling and dancing. Even Aty and Baba had seemed happy, despite it being just before Baba moved out; there was no tension, only peace.

Roya went to sleep dreaming about Katya placing her own flower crown on Roya's head at the end of the night, so that she had felt like a newly anointed fairy queen. She had liked it: being the queen.

But she woke up with dread in her stomach like a fat red brick. It was Monday. And she would not be going anywhere.

There was a knock on her door, and Aty entered. "Good morning, dokhtaram. I'm going to see Baba. Might be gone for most of the day. Can you just check in on the contractors to see if they need anything?"

"Okay," Roya said. Aty gave her a kiss on the head before leaving.

It took half an hour more for Roya to get herself out of bed, and then she went and sat down on the stairs between the third and fourth floors, staring up at the BunnytheBunny graffiti and the little brown rabbit ears that were painted atop both Bs. Thoughts were swirling in her mind, not even quite making sense to her as they urged her to go back downstairs and plop down on the little stoop in front of her door instead. When she did, she knew what she was waiting for. Or rather, who. And it didn't even take five minutes for them to appear.

The elevator door was pulled open, and Stefanie and Amin walked out. They were already deep in conversation, Amin in his B train shirt and jangling the coins in his pocket.

"So Original Annika danced ballet as a teen, right?" Amin said.

"Yes," Stefanie responded. "Pretty seriously. She was in a professional production of *The Nutcracker.*"

"From my research, it seems like even when the circus

troupe was gone, dancing and acrobatics still ran in the Petrov family," Amin said. "Maybe something like the time traveling."

"Maybe," Stefanie agreed. "And they were always attached to their stage name too, passing their last name of Petrov down from mother to daughter."

They were so absorbed in their conversation that they didn't even notice Roya. They would've walked right out the front door without acknowledging her if she hadn't stood up sharply.

"Hey!" she said, the snake in her stomach feeling like it was on fire.

Stefanie turned. "Roya."

"We were just headed to . . . ," Amin started.

"I know," Roya said. "That's why I'm here too." And then it was like the snake was the one slithering the words out of her mouth: "Aty changed her mind. She said I could go."

"She did?" Stefanie asked, a little dumbfounded. "When? Because when I spoke to her again last night, she still seemed dead set against it."

"Just this morning," Roya said, hardly believing how smooth and slippery this snake was. "We had a talk about it, and I made her realize I can handle this. She's spent all this time training me to think for myself and be independent. She knows I know how to be safe."

Stefanie squinted, and Roya stood up just a little taller.

Waiting, trying to breathe normally, trying not to dart her eyes or do anything that would give her away.

"Where is Aty?" Stefanie asked.

"With my dad," Roya said.

Stefanie cocked her head and looked at Roya. "I'm sorry, but I'm going to have to text her to ask."

"Oh, really?" Roya cast her eyes down. "I mean, I'm telling the truth, but okay. I understand."

Stefanie kept watching her as she took her phone out. She looked a little conflicted about typing the words even as she did it.

Roya waited.

And Stefanie and Amin did too, staring at Stefanie's phone.

Roya's heart was beating a little faster, but she tried not to let it show. Usually, Aty put her phone on silent when she visited Baba because he was often sleeping and she didn't want to disturb him. So maybe luck would be on her side.

They waited a couple more minutes, each second that ticked by making Roya surer that her mom would not see that message for a while. Far enough in the future for it to not matter.

The moment Stefanie looked up at Roya again, taking in her wide eyes and her calm stance, Roya knew that she had done it. She'd convinced Stefanie that she wouldn't lie.

"Okay," Stefanie said. "Let's go, then."

A Forbidden Trip

ON THE TRAIN RIDE OVER, Amin and Stefanie filled Roya in on their strategy for today. Since she'd been avoiding them, it was news to her that they'd decided against trying to talk to Original Annika if they saw her.

"It's too risky," Amin explained. "We still don't know what it would affect if we were to stop her from putting the coins in the machine. Look what happened with me just accidentally taking that note. Even the smallest change in the timeline could have huge consequences in the future."

"So what *is* the plan?" Roya asked.

"Observe for now," Stefanie said. "You two are excellent at that. Just see if there's anything we missed about how Annika traveled. And also see if you can find the Traveling Petrovs. We assume it would be Annika and Polina."

"We should be able to talk to *them*," Amin explained. "Since they have the barriers to protect them from messing up the main timeline, like your dad pointed out. They might have some more insight on how this all works."

The mention of Baba made Roya's stomach turn because he was, at this very moment, with Aty, and neither of them knew where Roya was. But she tried her best to ignore the feeling by nodding at Amin. "Got it."

There were more people at Coney Island than there had been the previous times. A couple of big camp groups were there, the kids' and their counselors' green shirts creating swathes of color throughout the amusement park.

"Hi, Roya!" a small voice called out from behind Roya. She turned to see that it was Bennett and Jonah, aka Bumblebee and Bear from 6D. They were in green shirts too, and gave Roya gap-toothed smiles.

"Hi, guys. Are you here with your camp?"

They nodded as their counselor called for them. "Bye!" they both yelled, and went to rejoin their group, who were waiting in line for the Wonder Wheel. Roya watched them, hardly believing there was a time when she was jealous of their camp adventures, when she didn't know that a huge, life-changing adventure was waiting just around the corner for her.

"Ready?" Amin asked, and Roya nodded. They walked up to Grandmother and clasped hands. Stefanie grabbed Roya's hand too, "just in case." But when Amin put the coins in, and the blip reset the world around them, neither was surprised—this time—that she wasn't there with them.

Roya and Amin took a minute to take in their surroundings. Coney Island in 1974 was just as colorful as the version they were used to, though everything seemed a little grittier, the rides rustier, and the boardwalk game booths grimier. The water gun booth offered up stuffed rabbits with big, painted lashed eyes that veered just a smidge into creepy territory.

The people around them were dressed in colorful clothes: lots of oranges and yellows, wide-legged jeans, and short denim shorts. Everyone's hair seemed bigger than usual too.

If her recorder had been working, Roya would have tried to capture the ambient noises of the park in 1974: the roller-coaster screams, boardwalk game dings, and family chatter were familiar, though there were no social media videos or text message pings to compete with them. Her split-second decision to leave with Stefanie and Amin had meant she'd left her journal behind too. Then again, she realized, Amin's echoic memory would be better than her journal anyway. She made a mental note to record him soon after they got back.

She and Amin stood in front of Grandmother now, waiting for Annika to show up. The younger version of her would look different from the version they'd seen last week. Stefanie had shown them as many photos of her as she could find, so they knew they were looking for blond hair instead of gray.

Amin gave a sharp intake of breath and grabbed Roya's arm because suddenly Annika had emerged from the crowd. She wore a sunshine-yellow dress that was nevertheless darker than her hair; her shade of blond was so light that it was closer to white anyway, so it was quite possible they would have easily recognized her even if Stefanie hadn't shown them the photos.

Annika took a deep breath, a coin already in her hand, but she didn't look nervous as she put it in the machine. And then—

"Oh!" Roya had not expected Annika's disappearance to happen so soon, before she'd put a second coin in.

She and Amin looked at each other and then ran up to Grandmother. "Ah," Amin said. "It only cost twenty-five cents back then."

Annika was gone, of course. Not a trace of her ever being there.

"Now we wait for Daria and see if the other Travelers come to help her out," Amin said. The two of them waited in silence one minute, then five, then ten. Roya's thoughts swirled, particularly as she watched a dad who seemed determined to win a creepy stuffed bunny for his daughter. There was an idea there, forming—just out of reach. What was it Amin had said about changing things for their families? And just as she thought she might be able to grasp at it, something in her peripheral vision shifted.

Roya turned to see a young redheaded woman standing in front of Grandmother, looking around in confusion.

"Daria's here!" Roya said, but before she could approach her, Amin had put a hand on her arm.

"I think we should wait and see if the other Travelers come," he said. "In case us talking to her first would mess that up from happening."

It was a more cautious approach than Roya would have taken on her own, but she nodded as they watched Daria take in her surroundings, look at Grandmother, and start to piece together that maybe she wasn't where she'd started out. Eventually, she began to walk toward the park exit. Roya and Amin followed her past the kiddie rides, which were much the same as they were fifty years in the future. Daria stopped at the entrance to look around, clocking the unusual clothes and the changed logo for the park.

She was standing by the ticket booth when she was approached by two women, one with platinum-blond hair, the other gray. "Daria?" the younger of the two said.

Daria's head turned. She stared at the two women for a moment, and then she gasped, getting out one word. "Mama?"

Annika nodded and came forward, arms wide open, until Daria flung herself into them.

A New Plan

ANNIKA HUGGED HER DAUGHTER AND smoothed out her hair as Daria cried softly into her shoulder. "It's okay, we're here now. Everything will be okay," she murmured in her ear.

Daria lifted her head to study her mother's face. "You look different from how I remember."

"She looks older, you mean," Polina cracked in her gravelly voice.

"Mama!" Annika said, but she was laughing.

Daria looked at the older woman in wonder. "Mama?"

"Babushka to you," Polina said, a smile warming her hardened features. "Which gives me the authority to ask: What in the world is this"—she touched Daria's spiky red hair—"and *this*?" She pointed to the small silver hoop in one of Daria's eyebrows.

"It's called an eyebrow ring," Daria said, a matching smile filling out her features. "Can I hug you now?"

Polina embraced her granddaughter, saying in her ear as she did, "Is this what people do to themselves in the future?"

"The future?" Daria asked as she leaned back to take a better look at her surroundings.

"Let's have a seat," Annika said, pointing to the familiar bench overlooking the ocean.

ROYA AND AMIN HOVERED ON the boardwalk nearby, close enough that they could hear Annika and Polina explaining everything to Daria without it being obvious that they were eavesdropping. They overheard them talking about the barriers and how they would be sticking together now, inviting Daria to move into their apartment with them. They also talked about how they'd brainstorm what stocks to invest in based on what Daria knew from her time.

"It'll take some getting used to," Annika said, her hand on her daughter's the whole time they spoke. "But it'll all be okay. We promise."

"And what about Sofia?" Daria asked. "And Katya? Will I see them again?"

"Sofia." Annika's voice wavered at the name, and she patted Daria's hand before she shook her head. "No, I don't think so. But Katya . . . is that your daughter?" she asked brightly.

"Sofia's daughter," Daria said. "I don't have any kids."

Annika looked at Polina, who nodded. "Then maybe she'll be the one to come," Polina said.

"She will," Roya finally said, stepping forward. She'd reached the end of her patience as a bystander. "Twenty-five years from now."

Polina looked over at her and asked curiously, "Who are you?"

"I'm Roya and this is Amin. We're . . . well, we're actually from Katya's time."

"2024," Amin clarified.

Annika and Polina gaped at Roya. "That far in the future?" Annika asked.

"2024," Polina repeated. "The final year on the original fortune."

Roya nodded. "Yes. And Grandmother told us we had one chance to save Katya. Only we're not sure what that means. We tried to have Katya come back with us in 1999, after you left." She pointed at Daria. "But it seems like we're the only ones who can travel backward *and* forward. She couldn't."

"You can do both?" Polina asked, nearly echoing her amazement at discovering the same information twenty-five years in the future.

"Wait a minute," Amin said, turning to Roya. "What you

just said about us being the only ones who can travel both ways. I wonder if that means . . ." He took a moment, as if he was still working it out in his head. "Maybe the only way to save Katya isn't to travel back with Original Katya but to stop Original Katya from ever traveling."

Roya blinked. "How would we do that? It doesn't seem like we can travel to the day when Katya disappeared again, can we?"

"Right," Amin said slowly, the wheels in his head turning. "And we're already past the dates when Daria and Annika traveled. But . . ." He looked at Polina. "How would it be if none of you traveled? If none of you ever traveled?"

"You mean if we all stayed together?" Polina asked. "In our own times?"

Amin nodded. "I don't know if it'll work, but if we can stop Original Polina from traveling, well, it would change things for *you*. The traveler versions of you who, probably, wouldn't exist. And also the money that you make from that"—he pointed at the lavender fortune—"couldn't happen."

Annika stared agape at Amin while Polina took the fortune from Daria's hand. "It was never really about the money. I had no idea I'd disappear from my own timeline, and Annika only came because she thought she might find me again," she explained. "The money means nothing compared to . . ." She looked over at her daughter and granddaughter. "Compared to getting to meet Sofia. And Katya. And whoever else has been in your life the past twentysomething years," she said to Daria, her eyes filling with joyful tears.

Annika frowned. "Mama . . ."

"Mama?" came another voice, and Roya and Amin turned to see a girl who looked about seven, with light brown hair, standing with a tall Asian man in a cream-colored shirt.

"Is this her?" the girl asked, pointing at Daria and smiling to reveal a gap where her front tooth should be.

Annika nodded. "Daria, meet Inessa." She took in a deep breath. "Your little sister."

24
The Message

"WELL, THIS COMPLICATES THINGS," **AMIN** said as they watched the second Petrov family reunion of the day taking place in front of them.

"But I guess it makes sense," Roya said. "We can't expect the Traveling Petrovs not to interact with anybody, just because they can't interact with their Original selves."

"So now I don't know what to do," Amin said, turning to Roya. "I wish we could talk to your dad."

"Me too," Roya said, but she didn't express the other thought that had been gnawing at her—ever since Amin took that note and affected the future by doing so. She wanted to sort it out for herself first before she let the words into the open, where they could be scrutinized and—possibly—shot down. "Maybe we should ask *them* what they want," Roya said, pointing to the Petrovs.

Daria and Inessa were hugging and chatting, and Annika

was watching them fondly. Polina, on the other hand, stood at a distance, frowning.

Roya and Amin approached her now. "Polina," Roya said, and the older woman turned to her, her eyes a little shiny.

"If my suggestion works," Amin said, "and we stop Original you from traveling. Well . . ." He paused there but pointed at Inessa and her dad, who was now being introduced to Daria by Annika.

Polina watched her family for a moment. "I never saw my husband again. And I never got to see my own baby grow up," she said quietly, nodding toward Annika. "And I'd want to."

"So you'd vote that we try to stop the traveling?" Roya asked, for confirmation.

Polina looked at the scene in front of her one more time but then turned away, whispering, "Yes."

"Mama," Annika hissed sharply, clearly having overheard. "How can you say that?" She placed a protective hand on Inessa's shoulder.

Polina looked down, ashamed. Inessa's dad seemed to sense a conversation happening that Inessa shouldn't overhear, so he pointed out a cotton candy vendor and started leading the girl toward it.

"I just feel . . . out of place," Polina said. "All the time. Like I missed a whole life."

"But we will literally miss a whole life if we don't travel." Annika pointed to Inessa and her dad.

"Yes," Polina said miserably before turning to Daria. "What do you think? Would you want to go back and never have come here?"

Daria looked back at Inessa. "I don't know. I miss Sofia. And Katya. The thought of never seeing them again . . ." She turned to her mother. "And never losing you at all . . ."

Polina was nodding, but Annika looked troubled. The three of them watched as Inessa picked out a sky-blue cotton candy and started insisting to her dad that they get one for her new sister too.

"Babushka," Daria said to Polina. "We can't."

Annika put her hand on Daria's shoulder in relief. Polina just looked away, staring out toward the ocean.

There was a moment of silence as they each pondered what this could mean for them.

Amin was the one to break it. "We have to get back. I promised my parents I wouldn't be gone over an hour without Stefanie."

Roya nodded. "Okay." She took a deep breath. This was the part where the idea that had been forming in the back of her mind was going to be put into action. "You go. I'll be there really soon."

Amin blinked at her. "What do you mean?"

"I have to go somewhere in this time period, but it won't take more than an hour. Tell Stefanie I'll be back by one."

Amin frowned. "What are you talking about, Roya. Go where?"

Roya sighed. She didn't think she'd be able to leave Amin without giving him an explanation, but there was a small part of her that had hoped anyway. He wasn't going to like this. "I have to find my great-uncle Khosrow. He lives in Bay Ridge where my dad lives now. I looked up the trains, and I have to take the N to the RR." She hoped mentioning the old subway lines that didn't run anymore would distract Amin enough to not ask the obvious question.

"Why are you visiting your great-uncle?" No such luck.

"I just . . ." Roya was running out of time and lies, so she stepped back into the truth like she was facing the glare of a spotlight. "I have to tell him about Baba getting sick in the future. If he *just* gets a checkup three years earlier, and they catch the cancer sooner, he'll probably be fine."

Amin frowned. "Roya! You can't!"

"Why?" Roya asked.

"The butterfly effect," Amin said. "Remember?"

"But we're trying to change everything for Katya's family," Roya pointed out.

"That's because Grandmother told us to," Amin said. "We're meant to change that timeline. But I wasn't supposed to take that note. And your dad—"

"Is *my* family," Roya said forcefully. "Can't you see? I have to try."

Amin hesitated. "But who knows what else you could change, Roya. Maybe he'd never meet your mom. Maybe you wouldn't be born. Maybe . . ."

But Roya didn't have any more time for Amin's *maybes*. She started to run down the rickety boardwalk, in the direction of the subway station. "You go back," she yelled over her shoulder. "I'll be there soon."

Amin shouted after her, but Roya couldn't hear him over the crowd. By the time she made it to the Nathan's building on the corner of Surf Avenue, he wasn't behind her anymore. *Good,* she thought. Hopefully he'd gone back and she'd join him soon. Act now, apologize later.

She waited at the corner for the light to change. The large subway station was just across the street, so close, but the light seemed to be taking a long time. She watched the people waiting in line for their hot dogs and fries at the restaurant. Further down, a muscled sword swallower performed outside a sideshow building while people gawked and clapped. Roya was so absorbed that she missed the light turning green by a couple of seconds. But then a honking horn jolted her out of her reverie, reminding her that she needed to focus.

She lifted one leg to place it over the lip of the sidewalk. Only she couldn't. Her leg was stuck in midair, like it had hit an invisible sheet of plastic right where the sidewalk ended. She picked up her other leg and tried again. Same thing.

All around her, people were crossing the street just fine, but none of her limbs would extend beyond the curb. She put her arm out, only to meet the same invisible resistance. This must be the barrier that the Traveling Petrovs talked about. She knew it, but it didn't stop her from continuing to try for three more light changes. Then she walked a couple of blocks down Surf Avenue and tried again. She still couldn't cross.

She kept walking until she reached Ocean Parkway itself, which she was unable to cross in any direction. She'd reached the end of her tether.

Roya screamed in frustration. A young girl looked at her curiously, but otherwise no one even glanced her way. There was so much noise here—from carnival barkers to car horns to the distant *clickety-clack* of wooden roller coasters—that it was normal for someone to be yelling loudly at any given moment.

Roya dejectedly made her way back toward Grandmother. When she reached the boardwalk, she noticed a young teenager, maybe about thirteen or fourteen, wearing a dingy, paint-stained tank top and sitting underneath a wall with two cans of spray paint, one yellow and one black, next to him. He appeared to be painting some animals on the wall. There was a large bee, a dog, and a rabbit.

The sight of the rabbit stopped Roya in her tracks. She stared at the boy as the ghost of an image played across her mind: the spray-painted words of BunnytheBunny, left on the Queen's staircase decades before.

"Hey!" Roya said, running up to the kid. An idea had formed, and though it seemed like a long shot, it was the only one that she had. She pointed at the can of black spray paint. "Can I borrow that? To write a message?"

The kid looked over at Roya. "Ain't you a little young to be on the wrong side of the law?"

"It's important," Roya said. "Please. It's a message for the future."

The kid hesitated and then shrugged. "I guess they're all messages to the future, one way or another. Be my guest."

Roya took the paint can and thought for a second. What was the best way to put this? She shook the can and pressed the button.

It was way harder to maneuver than she'd expected. She wanted to write the word Khosrow, her great-uncle's name, and she wanted to try to write it small so that maybe it wouldn't get painted over in the intervening forty years. But that was near impossible. It took her a full minute to get a large, shaky K up on the wall.

She turned back to the teen, whose own bee was looking at least recognizable. Clearly he had a lot more practice than she did. "What's your name?" she asked.

"Who's asking?" he shot back.

"Just me," Roya said. "I promise."

The boy hesitated for a moment before saying, "Kirby."

"Kirby, I'm Roya. Do you think you can help me write a message?" she asked.

"What's the message?" he asked.

"Can I write it down?" Roya asked, indicating the sketch-book and pen the kid had with him. He nodded.

Roya grabbed the pen and jotted: **Khosrow and Payman. P, see doctor in 2020.**

Kirby looked at her with his jaw dropped. "Is that, like, your tag or something?"

"Sorta," Roya said as she got hit with another brain wave. She reached into her pocket for the twenty-dollar bill that Aty had given her for the hardware store. "Here, take this. Write that in as many places as you can. Whenever you can." Maybe, just maybe, Amoo Khosrow or Baba would see it somewhere in Brooklyn someday and understand that the message was for them. It was such a long shot, so unlikely that Kirby would even do it, but it was the only inkling of hope she had.

Kirby stared at the money. "Is this real money? Where is this from?"

"It's real," Roya said truthfully, realizing that his twenties probably looked different from hers. Hopefully, someone would still accept it. "I have to go. Please do it. Please. It's for my dad. His life depends on it." Roya looked deep into Kirby's eyes, and he seemed to understand something in them because he nodded.

"Okay," he said.

"Thank you," Roya said, and gave him a huge grin before she dashed away down the boardwalk.

She was a sweaty mess by the time she got close to Grandmother. She wasn't expecting anyone to be there since there usually wasn't.

But there *was* someone there, with telltale tear tracks down his face.

"Where have you been?" Amin asked in a shaky voice.

"I told you to go without me," Roya responded.

"I tried," Amin said. "But apparently Grandmother will only let us travel together."

"Oh," Roya said. "Well, I'm here now. We can go."

Amin stared at her in disbelief. He looked like he wanted to say something else, but Roya grabbed his hand and ignored his gaze. Amin took out his quarter and plunked it in.

The world blipped, and they were standing in front of the modern, purple-clad Grandmother again.

"Roya," a stern voice called from behind, and they turned around to see Stefanie. She was frowning deeply as she waved her phone in Roya's direction. "Your mom texted me back."

25

The Liars

"I CAN'T BELIEVE YOU LIED to me," Stefanie said, just once and—all things considered—quite calmly.

That didn't stop Roya from feeling awful about it, though. "I'm sorry," she said. "But you wouldn't have let me come. And I had to."

"You lied to me too," Amin said, not quite as quietly. "And now I'm going to be in trouble with my parents."

Roya's temper flared, but she tried to tamp it down. "At least you'll have parents to be in trouble with tomorrow. Me, I'm not so sure. I had to try to change that."

"But we weren't supposed to affect anything else," Amin insisted. "The butterfly—"

"Enough with the stupid butterflies!" It was too late. The fire inside Roya was raging now. "This is *my dad* we're talking about here. My baba. You don't understand because you don't have to."

Amin stared at Roya for a few seconds and then looked away.

"Oh, Roya," Stefanie said, blinking at her with a sadness in her eyes that Roya hated just as much.

So Roya changed the subject. "Don't you want to know what happened with the Petrovs? What we found out?" Roya asked.

"Yes," Stefanie admitted. "But not right now. I need to take you back to your mom. She's incredibly upset, Roya."

Roya desperately wanted to see whether the graffiti was still there. "Can I just check on one thing?"

"No," Stefanie said firmly. "We're going back. Now." She put one arm around each of Amin's and Roya's shoulders and started steering them toward the subway station.

At least it'd be easy enough to find out if her dad ever got the message, Roya thought grimly. All she'd have to do is check in on him and see if he was still sick.

Stefanie kept the pace brisk as she walked them all to the station. None of them made eye contact with one another as they rode the F train back. Roya spent the time watching the familiar rooftops and gravestones pass by. She thought she might have seen a black *PAYM* scrawled on an old concrete wall, underneath layers and layers of other graffiti, but the train passed by too quickly for her to be sure. Her heart beat fast. She both did and didn't want to see her dad.

They were at their stop sooner than Roya would have liked. As they walked up to their building, she saw that Aty was waiting for them outside, looking more furious than Roya had ever seen her.

"Inside," she said to Roya. "Now."

Roya didn't look at Amin and Stefanie, or say goodbye. She just trudged into the building and through the door of 1A, followed closely by her mother. The door hadn't even properly shut before the yelling started.

"How could you do this?" Aty demanded. "How *could* you?"

"I'm sorry," Roya said. "But this was important."

"I trusted you," Aty said. "All these years I've trusted you so much. And this is how you repay me?"

"You've trusted me with lots of stupid things," Roya said. "Helping you out around here. Or making sure the construction workers are hydrated. But now, with this huge, important thing—"

"*This* is dangerous!" Aty replied.

"Lots of things can be dangerous," Roya spat back. "New York City can be dangerous. The subway can be dangerous."

"So you're saying I should never have let you do any of those things by yourself, either?" Aty asked.

"I'm saying you wanted me to be independent. And this is me being independent."

"Independently lying to me," Aty said. "And Stefanie."

"You lie too," Roya said.

"What? How?" Aty replied.

"We never say the truth about Baba, do we?" Roya asked. "Not you, not me, not him."

Aty stared at her daughter. "You want the truth. Okay. The truth is we're going to lose him. And do you think, for one second, that I can handle losing you too?"

"*That's* what I was trying to prevent," Roya said. "I'm the only one who can do something about it. So I did. Or at least I tried."

"What are you talking about?" Aty asked.

Roya shook her head. "It doesn't matter. I don't even know if it worked." She averted her eyes from Aty, only then noticing that the wall of their living room was painted a bland eggshell white instead of the bold mural of the girl and the pomegranate. There was an unfamiliar piece of furniture pushed up against it too, a desk of some sort.

Aty let out a deep, frustrated breath, and Roya looked back over at her. Aty's brow was furrowed and her arms were crossed. "I am so incredibly disappointed in you, Roya."

Roya couldn't help herself. "I'm disappointed in you too. You think you're such a cool mom. You think that by telling fortunes together or sending me out to pick up a can of paint, you're different from other parents. But you're just a liar. Everything is still on your terms. You just pretend and make me think it's not."

"Because you're *still* the child, Roya," Aty shouted. "*I'm* the parent."

"Convenient that you're acting like it *now*, Aty." Roya spat her name out, the harsh *t* feeling the opposite of a soft, rounded word like *Mom*—what Aty had never wanted Roya to call her.

"Go to your room," Aty said, for the first time Roya could ever remember. Her voice was quieter again, but it was like a lid on a roiling pot.

"Fine." Roya went to enter her room.

"Wait, Roya. Aty." Roya heard a voice by the door and turned around to see Stefanie. Aty evidently hadn't shut their apartment door at all, meaning half the building had probably heard their fight. *Great.* "I'm so sorry," Stefanie was saying. "This is my fault."

"It's not your fault," Aty immediately said to Stefanie. Roya felt a pang because even if the sentiment was mostly accurate, she also knew her mother would choose to blame Roya over one of the tenants. Aty's job always came first, and Roya found herself wondering why she seemed so happy to mother every single person in the building over her.

"No, it is," Stefanie said. "I wanted Katya back so badly, I forgot they were just kids, Aty. And for that, I'm so sorry. I won't be taking them back there again."

"But, Stefanie . . . ," Roya said, and wanted to add, *You have to.* Except she didn't know how Aty would react to that. So she settled for, "Amin and I still need to talk to you about what we learned today." She looked at Aty, waiting, but she wouldn't give her the satisfaction of asking for permission.

Aty looked back and forth between her daughter, Stefanie at the door, and Amin standing quietly just behind her. And then she sighed. "For Katya's sake, you can talk in the lobby. But you can't go farther than that. Not today."

She stepped aside so Roya could leave but then went inside to, Roya presumed, have her glass of tea. She didn't close the apartment door all the way.

The three of them stood on the steps for a moment until finally, Stefanie said, "Come. Tell me what happened."

"THERE'S A TRAVELER CHILD, THEN," Stefanie said after Roya and Amin had explained what they'd seen this time.

Roya and Amin nodded.

"So that means if we were somehow able to stop Polina from traveling at all, then Inessa wouldn't exist," Stefanie said.

"Right," Amin said. "Or, at least, we think so."

"But maybe not," Roya said. "Because if the barriers are there to protect the big events in the original timeline, well, maybe . . . somehow Inessa would be born anyway?"

Amin frowned. "But how? Her father isn't a traveler. He'd never meet Annika in her old life."

"Right," Stefanie said a little shakily. "So we shouldn't try to change it, but . . ." She had tears in her eyes. "But then Katya and I would never have our child, either."

"But the thing is," Roya said, "Grandmother *wants* us to change it. If not, why would she give us that fortune telling us we have one chance to do it? That's what you said, Amin. Right?"

"Yes," Amin said. "She's the portal. I think she's calling the shots."

"So it's settled," Roya said confidently. "We have to stop the cycle of Petrovs traveling in order to get Katya back. And trust that whatever happens as a result was meant to happen."

Stefanie hesitated for a moment. "Okay," she said. "Or at least, *I* have to try to get Katya back. I'm sorry, but you two can't come."

Roya frowned. "But we have to. You can't go through."

Stefanie shook her head. "I can't go against the wishes of your mother, Roya. I'm sorry. And, Amin, I shouldn't be dragging you into this, either. You're just kids."

Roya was really starting to hate that line.

"I'll figure something out," Stefanie continued. "In the meantime, I think both of you should go home."

Amin was already nodding and standing up. Roya was

reluctant to unquestioningly follow what an adult was telling her to do, but she stood up too.

They muttered their goodbyes, and she returned to her apartment.

As she expected, Aty was sitting in her armchair with her tea. She wasn't reading or doodling, though, just staring out into space.

A part of Roya wanted to tell her everything: About meeting Kirby. About the possibility that Baba was okay.

But then she realized something. If Aty had just said that they were going to lose her dad, then . . . she couldn't have changed anything in the timeline, could she?

Roya's heart was sinking, almost as fast as her hopes. But she knew she had to be sure.

"Is it okay if I FaceTime Baba?" she asked quietly.

Aty looked at her and gave one short nod before turning away.

Roya's heart pounded as she took the tablet and navigated over to her dad's name. She hesitated for one moment before hitting the green button.

Her own face stared back at her as her dad's phone rang. She was surprised at how shiny her eyes were. She didn't even know she was close to tears until she saw it on the screen.

Baba accepted the call, and the screen was black for a

millisecond, just like Grandmother's blip, before his face appeared.

He was wearing a thin white tank top, thin enough that Roya could see the IV port sticking out of his chest. He looked just as gaunt as the last time she had seen him. He smiled at the sight of her face, but all Roya wanted to do was cry. It hadn't worked. It had all been for nothing.

"Hi, azizam," Baba said.

"Baba, I'll . . . call you back," Roya said hurriedly, and pressed the red button right before she dissolved into tears.

26

The Sea Doctor to the Rescue

ROYA KEPT TO HER APARTMENT for the rest of the week. It looked as drab as she felt. All the walls were white, not just the one in the living room. There were none of Aty's murals, not even the two sisters on a magic carpet. Roya wondered about it a little, but her funk was too deep to leave much room for curiosity.

Roya did the few chores her mom asked of her, but, other than that, there was no wandering around the building scouting for new podcast material, and definitely no seeking out Amin or Stefanie. They seemed to be avoiding her too.

On Thursday, she got a comment from one of her Danish subscribers that she put through Google Translate. They asked why there hadn't been a new episode in a few weeks. It was nice that someone cared, but it wasn't enough to make her want to record anything. Katya was still missing. Her dad was still sick. Nothing seemed like it was going to have a satisfying conclusion.

On Friday, she dutifully went and visited Baba, and he dutifully, if a bit half-heartedly, chastised her for lying to her mom.

"I know, Baba," Roya said dully.

"Okay, good," Baba said, and tried to wait a respectful thirty seconds before eagerly asking what happened during their last trip. "Or do you want to FaceTime Amin so you can tell me together?"

"No," Roya said, a little too quickly, and before her dad could ask about it, she launched into the story. "We're in a bit of a sticky situation." Roya told him about the Traveling Petrovs, particularly Inessa and how saving Katya could wind up erasing her. "We're hoping that her existence might be one of those immutable events you mentioned. But then Amin pointed out that Inessa's parents would never meet without the traveling, so how could that be?"

"That is a sticky situation," Baba agreed.

Roya nodded, a lump in her throat stoppering any words she might say about their own family. "Anyway, it's out of our hands now. Stefanie has to see what she can do about it." She shrugged. Maybe if she pretended she didn't care, soon enough it would become true.

Baba looked at Roya sitting on the couch that, up to a year ago, would have had her legs swinging. Now they reached the floor. "Maybe I can talk to your mother," he started.

"Don't bother," Roya said. "It's not worth getting into a fight over."

Baba opened his mouth and then closed it, frowning at the sight of his daughter slumped on the couch.

"Do you want me to order lunch?" Roya asked after a long stretch of silence.

"Sure," Baba said, and handed over his phone. "Get whatever you're in the mood for. I'm sure I'll find something to pick from the menu." Roya knew that meant he had no appetite. She took the phone grimly while he closed his eyes.

She was listlessly looking through restaurant options when a question nagged at her mind, a question she had to ask even though she could already guess at its answer. "Baba?"

"Hmmmm," he said without opening his eyes.

"When you were growing up, did you ever . . . I don't know. See your name around the city? In graffiti?"

Baba's eyes popped open. "How did you know that? I thought all those tags were long gone."

Roya's jaw dropped. It had worked? But then she looked at Baba's frail frame: it hadn't really. "What did they say, the tags?"

"My name and Amoo Khosrow's. I always thought it was a pair of kids. But I'd never met anyone here with our names before, so it was fun to imagine this other Payman sailing around with another Khosrow and the Sea Doctor. Sounded almost like an ancient Persian epic poem."

"Sailing around with the Sea Doctor?" Roya repeated. "Sea, like the ocean? S-e-a?"

"Yes," Baba said. "Sometimes there would be an illustrated sea creature, like an octopus or a large fish. And once I saw it written on a picture of a submarine: 'The Sea Doctor 2020.'"

Roya almost burst into tears again. Had she been so careless when she quickly scrawled out the message for Kirby and not checked that her handwriting was legible? He had read it "*sea* doctor," instead of "*see* doctor." All this time . . . wasted.

"Anyway, your mother took that and ran with it, of course," Baba said, a faint smile on his lips.

"What do you mean?" Roya asked.

"Her books," Baba said. He gestured toward the bookshelf. Roya looked over at it. It looked the same as always, except—wait, what was up with the bottom shelf? Didn't it used to be filled with textbooks like the others? Now it seemed to contain a series of slim paperbacks. Roya walked over and slipped one off the shelf. No, not just paperbacks: graphic novels. *Khosrow and the Sea Doctor, Volume 3: A Djinn Out of Water,* its title proclaimed. And then, underneath that, *By Aty Zonouzi.* Roya flipped through the pages, recognizing her mother's distinctive illustrations punctuated by metallic paint. "Aty . . . ," she said softly.

"That's where her Khosrow came from," Baba said. "I mean, the seed of it. I just told her about the graffiti. The rest was your mother's own imagination."

Roya looked up at her father. "So she's a published author?"

Baba looked at Roya a bit strangely. "Of course she is. For almost your whole life."

Roya rubbed her hand on the cover. Maybe that's why the apartment seemed different, less colorful. Undoubtedly, that's why Aty herself had seemed a little different too. She'd channeled her talents into something bigger than their walls.

"Anyway, how did you know about the graffiti?" Baba asked. "It's been so long since I've seen that tag that I actually forgot I once told your mom about it."

"Just something I heard. From Aty," she said. There was a strange feeling in her heart, like the streaks of blues and yellows making up the ocean on the cover of Aty's book. Roya was blue—sad that she had failed in rescuing her father. And yet, there was a bright spot: maybe somehow she had rescued something for her mother.

WHEN ROYA GOT HOME FROM Baba's, she couldn't help but be curious about this version of Aty. Now that she looked around their apartment more closely, she noticed that while their living room bookshelf still had the copy of *The Divan of Hafez* on the bottom shelf, it was otherwise overflowing with copies of Aty's Sea Doctor series. Roya also discovered what that new piece of furniture was: a proper drafting table. In the evenings, Aty was no longer doodling in a sketchbook while she read, but rather set up at her inclined desk and drawing on thick, loose sheets of paper, her glass of tea still beside her. Roya couldn't stop sneaking peeks of her while she was sketching.

"It's almost like you've never seen me draw before," Aty observed.

And Roya supposed she could tell her that in the timeline

she was most used to, she hadn't—at least, not like this. But telling Aty about how she'd potentially changed the course of her life fifty years ago—but hadn't been able to change the course of her dad's—well, it was too big a conversation to have. Especially with someone she wasn't really speaking to.

Roya was avoiding Amin too. She saw him heading out a couple of times with his mom or dad, presumably to the restaurant or library, but she purposefully hid in the stairwell or went back into her apartment until he left. She didn't think he'd quite forgiven her for leaving him stranded at Deno's, unable to travel through Grandmother on his own. But she hadn't quite forgiven him for not understanding why she'd had to do it, either.

Even so, on Monday morning, Roya couldn't help but sit on her stoop. She was waiting for Stefanie and Amin, knowing they were likely going to Coney Island again. Eventually, the elevator door opened and Stefanie stepped out. She gave Roya a wave and a sad sort of smile as she walked past.

"Where's Amin?" Roya asked.

Stefanie shook her head. "I can't involve the two of you anymore."

"But I don't think you can go through without us," Roya said.

Stefanie tried to smile. "Worth a try, right?"

Roya didn't think so. It was already near the end of August. Before they knew it, summer would be over, and the amusement park wouldn't be open on Mondays at all. Besides, if Amin's theories were correct, today might be the one and only day the portal to 1949—Polina's year of traveling—was open. Roya was scared they were letting their one chance of rescuing Katya slip away. But what else could she do? Stefanie couldn't take her, because Aty wouldn't let her go.

While Roya waited for Stefanie to return, she took out her recorder for the first time in a week and recorded a short bit about the graffiti and how it had changed Aty's life. But it didn't feel complete. She needed Amin to help fill in more details about what they'd found out when they saw the Petrovs in 1974.

Stefanie returned a little after one in the afternoon, looking exhausted and frustrated. Even though Roya could guess the reason why, she still asked what had happened.

"Just as you expected," Stefanie said. "It didn't work, of course."

There was the sound of footsteps on the stairs, and suddenly Amin was there too, his face flushed with anticipation. He must have been sitting in the stairwell one floor up, also waiting for Stefanie. "Can you tell us exactly what you did?"

"I must have put in fifty dollars' worth of coins," Stefanie said dully. "For whatever reason . . ." She trailed off.

"Only we can go," Roya finished for her.

"Together," Amin added, and he caught Roya's eye. At first, Roya thought he might be making a dig about how she'd stranded him last time. But then, as she looked at him in his L subway shirt, she realized that she knew him. He was not someone who said one thing and meant another. He was just stating a fact.

"Yes," Roya said, nodding. "Together. And Grandmother told us we have one chance." She looked at her door, at the 1A that she and Aty had stuck on there together, and offered up a fact of her own. "I have to talk to my mom."

The Divan of Aty

ROYA KNEW THREE THINGS. ONE: She had to help Katya. Even if she couldn't affect anything about her dad's life, this was something she'd been given a chance to change, so she *had* to. Two: She wouldn't get away with lying to her mom again. But that second point almost didn't matter, because the third, and most important, point was that she needed to talk to Aty. For real.

She walked into their apartment and found her in the living room, poring over the top page from the legal pad they kept outside their door. Aty took it down twice a week, on Mondays and Thursdays, to look over the tenants' non-urgent issues and figure out whom she needed to schedule, where, and when.

From the doorway, Roya observed her for a split second. Aty was writing down appointments on the large calendar splayed across their coffee table. There was a house rule that this was important, focused work and that Aty shouldn't be disturbed.

But Roya knew that what she had to say was important too.

"Aty," Roya started, and waited until Aty looked up, small concentration lines wrinkling her forehead. "I know you're busy, but we need to talk. And we don't have much time."

Aty paused for a moment. "What is it?" She still held her pen poised over the legal pad, but at least she was looking at Roya.

Roya took in a deep breath to bolster her courage. "I have to go to Coney Island to help Katya. For whatever reason, Amin and I are the only ones who can do it. And Grandmother said we have this one chance. I think this might be the last day we can go because this would take us back to the first year the Petrovs ever time-traveled."

Aty sighed as she put down her pen and closed her eyes. "You know I care about Katya as much as you do," she said, and then opened her eyes to look at her daughter. "But you're just a kid, Roya. Even if I haven't always treated you like one."

"But how you've treated me, Aty"—Roya swallowed—"it's like . . . you trust me to make my own decisions."

"I've left you alone too much," Aty said. "I haven't parented you enough. I know that."

Roya shook her head. "You're a great mom."

Aty's eyes were a little glossy. "You think so?"

"Of course," Roya responded, and then, looking closer at

Aty's face, realized—maybe for the first time—how much what she said here would matter to her. "Most of my classmates aren't allowed to do what I am."

"But maybe that's exactly why I shouldn't let you do it, either," Aty said.

"What's right for someone else may not be what's right for you," Roya said gently. "Aren't you always saying that?"

Aty raised one eyebrow at Roya, looking more like herself as she did so. "Yes, but I never got the impression you were listening to me."

Roya shrugged. "I'm always listening to you. Even if I don't act like it. I'm also sorry about what I said. I love you."

"I love you too, Roya jaan," Aty said.

"You've always trusted me, Aty," Roya said. "Please. You have to trust me with this. I know it's the right thing for me. I know it. Here." She put her hand on her stomach, where her mom always put her own hand when she told her to trust her gut.

Aty hesitated. "I'm just scared," she finally said in a small voice. "Of something going wrong. Of losing you too."

Roya nodded. "But being scared is not a reason to avoid something."

Aty laughed. "What, have you been writing down all my sayings?"

"The Divan of Aty," Roya replied. "It's very useful."

"Especially when you're going to throw them all in my face to get your way," Aty replied with a smirk.

"Naturally," Roya said.

Aty took in a deep breath, and they stood looking at each other, their eyes conveying words that remained unspoken but were still understood. "Okay," Aty said, nodding once. "You can go. But I'm coming with you."

"What about them?" Roya indicated the legal pad in front of Aty, her eyes catching on the long list of apartment numbers and grievances that went down the page, all in different handwriting.

"For once, they can wait," Aty said firmly. "I'm going to text Management and tell them there's an emergency." She brought out her phone and quickly fired off a text. She pocketed it before a response could come through. "Let's go."

29

All Together Now

ROYA GRABBED THE ORIGINAL LAVENDER fortune from her bookshelf along with her recorder. Even though she knew it wouldn't work in the past, there was still something comforting about carrying it with her. And then, before she could think too hard about it, she grabbed a black paint pen from a stash on Aty's drafting table. Then she followed Aty out of the apartment as they went to knock on Stefanie's door.

"We're going to try one more time," Roya told Stefanie excitedly, and watched as her eyes lit up.

"Really?" she asked, looking to Aty for confirmation. Aty nodded.

"Let's go get Amin," Roya said, and they walked downstairs to collect him too.

His front door was slightly ajar, so they got a peek of him

sitting at his dining room table, looking over his timeline, before Roya got his attention by calling his name.

"What's going on?" he asked when he saw everyone gathered at his door.

Mrs. Lahiri came out of the kitchen to see what all the noise was about. "Can Amin come with us to Coney Island?" Roya asked.

Amin's eyes lit up. "You can go?" he asked Roya.

She nodded, reaching out to squeeze her mom's hand.

Aty looked over at Amin's mom. "Do you want to come too, Rimi?"

Mrs. Lahiri looked at the group and then at the red-spiced ladle in her hand. "Um, you know what . . . ? Give me a few minutes."

She went back into the kitchen, and they heard the sounds of beeping, a sink running, and the clanging of items being put in a dishwasher before she emerged again, her apron off. "I'm ready," she said, and the five of them marched down the stairs and out of the building.

"So tell us how all this works exactly," Aty said as their F train rolled out of the station. "Today is your last chance to go?"

"I'm not exactly sure, but I think so," Amin said. "Because today would take us back to 1949, and that was the first year one of the Petrovs traveled."

"Ah. Polina's time," Mrs. Lahiri said, and laughed when she

saw Roya looking at her in surprise. "Amin likes to share all his big projects. Like his timeline."

Roya felt the weight of the recorder in her pocket, thinking about how she hadn't been sharing much at all with her parents lately. Maybe that ought to change once this adventure was over. Maybe she could even let them listen to an episode of her podcast.

The midafternoon sun was high and brazen in the sky when they exited the station at Coney Island, but there was a slight breeze in the air too, the tiniest hint at summer's end. It wouldn't be long before the Atlantic Ocean would be too cold to wade into and the beach blankets and umbrellas would be replaced by coat-clad couples going for a chilly seaside walk.

Roya glanced at the empty bench where she had sat with Katya and the rest of her family, and she let herself visualize sitting there with Katya again—now, in the present day. Manifestation.

The five of them walked down the boardwalk, through Deno's entrance, and underneath the *Thrills This Way* tunnel until they got to Grandmother.

"So this is the famous Grandmother?" Aty asked, staring into the glass eyes.

"This is her," Roya said.

"She looks smaller than I imagined," Aty confessed.

"Unassuming," Mrs. Lahiri chimed in.

"Yes, that's the word. Unassuming," Aty agreed.

Roya had once thought that too, but now she knew better. Grandmother seemed to know the ins and outs of the whole world—or, at least, the corner of it she'd been occupying for the past century.

"Ready?" Roya asked Amin, who was already pinching two quarters from his pocket.

Amin nodded and grabbed Roya's hand.

"Be safe," Mrs. Lahiri said as she gave Amin a kiss.

Roya turned around to take one last look at her mom. Aty smiled and winked. "Ditto."

Roya smiled back and then turned around just as Amin's second coin clinked into the machine, bringing with it the familiar blip.

The Final Chance

THE WONDER WHEEL LOOMED ABOVE them, as always, with its line of people waiting to ride. Many of them were wearing hats, all of them dressed in clothing that seemed fancier than anything Roya had seen in an amusement park before. There was a redheaded kid, probably not much older than Roya or Amin, working at one of the game booths, calling people in to try their luck at throwing a heavy ball into the gaping mouth of a painted clown. Anyone who got it in three tries won a tin whistle as a prize—which the kid was happily blowing into in demonstration.

And of course, Grandmother was there, the Guardian of the Wheel. She was dressed differently again and looked a little more sinister than Roya and Amin had ever seen her. *This is your last chance,* she seemed to be saying with her unseeing glass eyes.

Roya and Amin looked at one another. "We wait?" Amin asked.

Roya nodded.

They stepped away from the machine and observed the world around them. This was the first date on Grandmother's card and, quite possibly, the last chance Roya would have to travel back in time—to see this world in vibrant color instead of as a black-and-white image in a history book. She pointed out a woman in a particularly large, flamboyant straw hat that took the shape of a multicolored parrot, complete with real feathers.

"Bet you never saw anything like that in the books at the library," Roya said to Amin.

"A photo could never do that justice," Amin agreed as they watched the shimmering feathers swaying in the light.

"Step right up, step right up. Can you make the clown eat crow? You there! The pair of you!" Roya and Amin turned around to see that the redheaded kid was pointing at them. "What do you say? Want to try your luck? Just a penny for three tosses." He was offering them a heavy brown ball with a black crow painted across it.

Roya and Amin looked at each other.

"I actually have a penny," Amin said softly, patting his

pocket. "Since I wasn't entirely sure what kind of change Grandmother would need in order for us to get back."

"Want to give it a try?" Roya asked.

Amin stared into the booth, sounding wistful when he said, "It's not really part of the plan. . . ."

Roya took in his worried face and tried to understand. "The butterflies, right?"

"Yeah," Amin said. "I'm just scared of what I might change."

"But, Amin," Roya said gently. "Anything you do at any time could change the future. And that's not a bad thing, is it? You're a part of this world. You have as much right to affect things as anyone else."

"But what if I affect it the wrong way?" Amin asked.

"How would you know if throwing that ball would be right or wrong unless you do it?" Roya asked. "Taking your mom's note? The graffiti? I'm starting to think the future is unknown no matter what. Even to us time travelers."

Amin looked over at the booth again, clearly weighing Roya's words. "I do *want* to try it," he said softly.

The redheaded kid, sensing he was about to reel in a paying customer, called over to him enthusiastically, "Listen to your friend! Don't miss the chance to own one of these beauties!" He blew hard in his whistle, making its shrill tone sound positively gleeful.

"Come on," Roya laughed. "How can you refuse that offer? Besides, what did Grandmother's first fortune tell us? 'A redheaded person will prove a great friend'?"

Amin smiled, then pulled himself up to his full height before he walked over and handed a new penny to the boy.

"Gee, that's the shiniest one I ever saw," the boy said, but thankfully put it in his till without looking too closely at its year of minting.

Amin picked up one of the balls and practiced moving it from one hand to the other, getting a feel for its weight.

"The trick," the redheaded boy offered helpfully, "is to aim for the tonsils." He pointed at the back of the clown's black maw, which, sure enough, sported a painted red W shape.

"That's actually the uvula," Amin said. "Not the tonsils."

"Really?" the boy asked, squinting at the picture. "You sure?"

"I'm sure," Amin said.

"Huh. I'll have to tell my uncle. He's the one who painted it. U-vula, you say?"

Amin nodded.

"All right, then," the boy said. "Aim for the uvula."

Amin took in a deep breath, wound his arm back, and threw the ball. It overshot, sailing above the clown's head.

"Try again," the boy said, handing over another ball.

This time, Amin took an extra few seconds, moving through the arm motions without actually letting go of the ball. When he finally did it for real, it sailed through the clown's mouth.

"There you go!" the boy said enthusiastically as Roya clapped. Amin grinned wide as the boy handed him a tin whistle.

"Thanks," Amin said.

"Thanks for playing!" the boy said.

Amin placed the cord of the whistle around his neck and looked down at his prize, smiling shyly. It was then that Roya made a decision. She needed to right something from her past, but not via time travel. Via something much simpler: an apology.

"Amin," she started. "I'm sorry."

Amin looked up from his whistle. "What for?"

"Last time we came, I should've told you what I wanted to do from the beginning. That I wanted to try to change things for my dad. It's just that I thought you might stop me."

Amin thought for a second. "Well, for what it's worth, I probably would have. Messing with time is scary, and Grandmother seems pretty strict about us only changing this one thing."

"I know," Roya said. "But it *is* my dad."

Amin nodded. "If it were me . . . I probably would've tried too."

"It didn't help, anyway. It didn't make him better. But there was an unintended consequence that, actually, might have been a good thing." Roya told Amin about Aty and her books.

"Wow," Amin said. "You think they were in the library when I went this week?"

"Possibly," Roya said. "But I think . . ." She reached into her pocket and took out the paint pen. "I think I should try again. Maybe it won't help Baba, but maybe Aty . . . that felt right for her, to have her books. I wanted to tell you this time, though. Not just run off."

Amin looked at the pen and took a moment. And then he smiled. "Thank you for not running off." Roya realized that's all she needed from him. Not approval but his understanding that she felt she had to do this, whether he agreed with it or not.

Two people walked between them and Roya didn't pay them much attention. It wasn't until they walked toward Grandmother that Roya took a closer look. These weren't just any two people; it was a young blond woman walking with an older woman who was pushing a baby in a carriage.

Roya and Amin looked at each other and said at the same time, "Polina!"

Which, of course, caused the younger woman to immediately turn to them. "Yes?" she said, looking confused at the sight of two strangers who somehow seemed to know her name.

This was it—their final chance had arrived.

THE YOUNG BLOND WOMAN PEERED at Roya and Amin. "Do I know you?" she asked. Roya was struck by how much she looked like Katya, the same blue eyes and oval face.

"No," Roya said. "But also . . . yes."

"Some version of you knows us," Amin added. "In the future."

Polina looked over at Natasha.

"Maybe some sort of sideshow?" Natasha said in a thick Russian accent. She was tall and thin and, even at her age, had the posture of the acrobat that Roya knew she once was. "You trying to get us to play game?" Natasha gestured to the carnival games surrounding them.

Roya wasn't surprised she asked, since the redheaded barker wasn't much older than her or Amin. But she shook her head. "We're actually here to prevent you from using that." She pointed at Grandmother, who seemed to have a challenging gleam in her glass eyes. A trick of the light . . . probably.

Natasha looked at Grandmother and then back at Roya. "Why? That is very good machine."

Roya shook her head. "No, it's not. Maybe it gave you a great fortune last time. But this time, it won't. In fact, it'll make you disappear." She looked into Polina's eyes. "And you'll never get to see her grow up." She pointed at the little hand that was sticking out of the old-fashioned baby stroller.

Polina looked startled as she gave a small, nervous laugh. Natasha stepped in between her and the kids. "All right, enough. I do not know what your trick is. Unless you want to use machine first. You can go before us if you want." She gave an impatient wave of her hand.

"You have to believe us," Amin said passionately. "I know it sounds impossible, but we're from the future. And we've seen your family and how every Petrov who's used the machine has disappeared."

"That's ridiculous," Natasha said. "I have used the machine and I have not disappeared."

"Everyone except you," Amin said.

"Annika!" Roya said. "Your baby is named Annika, isn't she?"

Polina's eyes widened. "How do you know that?"

"Because," Roya said gently, "like he said, we *are* from the future. And if you use that machine now, you will disappear from Annika's life. You won't be able to see her grow up."

Polina looked frightened, and Roya felt bad saying the words that made her feel that way. But it was also the truth, and their only job right now was to try and prevent her from traveling so that they could stop the chain altogether.

Natasha didn't look frightened, however. She looked angry. "I do not know why you are saying all this, but go. Now. Or I will find police."

But Roya wasn't scared of the police. What she was scared of was failing Katya. After all this, she couldn't stand the thought that she wouldn't have been able to rescue anybody. She looked at Polina with imploring eyes. "Your baby is named Annika and your mother, that's Natasha. She was married to . . ." She looked over at Amin, who definitely knew the family tree better than she did.

"Ivan." Amin picked up where Roya had left off. "You came from Russia in 1916 as part of the Traveling Petrovs. You were both acrobats. But then you stopped traveling when you got pregnant with Polina. And Ivan got a job working here for a bit, helping to build the Wheel. He also helped build Grandmother for you. He made it look like *your* grandmother, so, in a way, she's a Petrov too. That's why we think your family can travel."

Natasha turned to Polina. "They must work for park and know all this," she said in her low, gravelly voice, which Roya noticed was similar to Polina's in the future.

"But what about Annika's name?" Polina asked.

"They must have overheard us saying it," she said. "If they don't want us to use Grandmother, there must be good reason. A valuable reason." Natasha looked at the kids and narrowed her eyes. "Step aside," she said.

Amin did as she asked almost without hesitation because, Roya realized, he was so used to obeying instructions, particularly from grown-ups. But if there's one thing Aty had drilled into Roya, it was to think for herself.

"No," Roya said, just as firmly as Natasha. "Listen, we can tell you more. Ivan built Grandmother with a man named Cornelius Lank, who, we think, might actually be Cornelius Lanczos. He was a mathematician and physicist, and, well, maybe he really *did* figure out time travel. And when you came here twenty-five years ago, Grandmother gave you a fortune that told you to invest in radio, and she told you to send your daughter here, today, plus listed three other dates in the future. Look."

Roya reached into her pocket and took out the original lavender fortune.

Natasha looked at it, frowning. And then glanced up at Roya.

"So. You could've put that fortune in there and have another copy. Or . . ." She took another suspicious look at Roya. "Your family could have. Especially if you work for park."

Roya shook her head. "We don't." She turned to Polina. "That machine? It won't give you a fortune. It'll make you go back in time. So you'll be able to create your own fortune for your family. But there's a price to pay. And the price is her." She pointed at the baby. "Then she'll grow up, come here on that second date listed on the card. And *she'll* disappear. And her daughter. And then her granddaughter. And there will be so many mothers missing from your daughters' lives, and trust me, you don't want that. It's not worth any amount of fortune. You told us that yourself, Polina. Twenty-five years from now." Roya's voice was becoming more impassioned, laced with something that sounded like tears. "Please. You have to trust us. You just have to."

Polina looked at Roya's face and down at the lavender fortune she was clutching before she turned to Natasha. "Mama. What if we . . . don't?"

"Are you joking?" Natasha said sharply. "She's just a child. And she's making things up. You can't believe her."

"But I do," Polina said quietly.

"Come back tomorrow," Amin implored. "Come back and get a fortune tomorrow."

"But that won't do anything," Natasha said. "It will be regular fortune. I know. I've gotten almost a hundred of them since the first time." She turned to Polina. "They're trying to stop us from getting money so they can keep it for themselves. But we need it, myshka. You know we do."

Polina glanced at Roya and Amin and then down at her daughter, who gave a gurgled coo. "I can't. What if they're right? I can't lose Annika. What if you had lost me?"

Natasha opened her mouth, still looking angry, but then she closed it again, peering closer into the face of her granddaughter. "What they say sounds impossible," she murmured.

"But the whole thing is impossible, Mama," Polina said. "Even Grandmother's original fortune . . . it's impossible." Polina grabbed Natasha's hand. "Let's go home," she said. "We'll figure something out about the money together. Okay?"

Natasha gave one last long look toward Grandmother and then let out a big sigh. "It is your decision," she finally said as she turned away, pushing the baby pram farther from Roya and Amin.

Polina hung back. "Thank you?" she said almost like a question.

Roya smiled. "Have a good life with your daughter and your family. We know you will."

Polina nodded, before hurrying along after her mother

and the baby. Amin and Roya watched her get absorbed into the crowd before Amin turned to Roya. "We did it," he said in wonder. "We stopped the time travel."

"We did," Roya said, smiling. "And now . . . just this one last thing." She took out the paint pen.

Amin looked at it for a moment before nodding. "Let's go."

Roya knew exactly where she wanted to go: the same spot Kirby had done the first graffiti. It felt like it was the right place.

She knelt beside the wall and wrote it two ways this time. **Khosrow and the Sea Doctor** and **Payman Alborzi, go to the doctor in 2020.** She didn't think the second message would make it through, but she knew she had to try one last time. And then she added one final note: **Love, Roya.**

When she was done, she and Amin went back to Grandmother. There was no sign of Natasha and Polina.

"You think they really left?" Roya asked. "That they won't come back once we're gone?"

"I think you convinced Polina," Amin said. "At least, I hope so."

"There's only one way to find out for sure," Roya said, her heart speeding up.

Amin nodded. "Let's go home."

This Time Around

"WHERE ARE THEY?" AMIN ASKED, looking around them.

They seemed to have made it back to the pleasant, breezy day in their own time. There were a lot of people around, dressed normally and with their smartphones in hand, with three noticeable exceptions: no Stefanie, Aty, or Mrs. Lahiri.

Roya's brain reeled. "If Polina never traveled, then we would have no reason to travel either, so . . . maybe they were never here?" She looked excitedly over at Amin. "This might be a good sign that it worked."

"Yes . . ." Amin allowed a slow smile to appear before his eyebrows knitted together in a worried expression. "Though if that's true, my parents are going to be so mad I'm here by myself."

"Not entirely by yourself," Roya said as she put out her hand. "Come on. Let's get back to the Queen."

The whole subway ride home, both Roya and Amin looked

for signs that something might have changed other than the adults missing from the park, but there weren't any. According to Amin, every billboard was still the same.

The Queen looked the same too: same willow tree, same black wrought-iron fence surrounding the grassy area in the front, same pink and purple flowers in the hanging planters that Aty used to spruce it up in the summer. The sun was getting lower in the sky, tinting the windows of the top floor a golden orange.

Roya and Amin approached the front door, and Roya used her key to get in. So far, the building seemed extra quiet, maybe even eerily so. No babies waddling around in the lobby, or someone coming back with a cart full of groceries, or one of the older tenants leaving with a nurse for a walk.

"Should we check 3G?" Amin asked. Katya and Stefanie's apartment. It seemed so final, whatever the answer was, but Roya nodded.

There was the sound of a door opening, and Roya turned to see that it was the one to her own apartment. Aty was leaving it. She was dressed differently than Roya had ever seen her: a green dress and sparkly sandals, no yoga pants and T-shirt; she didn't look like she was about to go do work around the building.

She started as she noticed Roya in the lobby.

"Hi," she said. "What are you doing here?"

"What do you mean?" Roya asked.

"Why aren't you at camp?" Aty asked, puzzled.

"Camp?" Roya blinked and then looked at Amin excitedly. She'd never gone to summer camp before. They must have done it. They must have changed at least some things.

"Who dropped you off?" Aty was frowning now as she looked at Amin. "Mr. Lahiri?"

Roya's mind was racing. So Aty knew Amin and Mr. Lahiri, meaning they'd still moved here.

"Yes," Roya lied, because it was the easiest thing to do at the moment. "Aty, we were wondering, is Katya here?"

"Katya?" Aty asked, looking at them blankly.

Roya gulped. She was about to open her mouth to speak when the elevator door opened behind them.

She turned to see Stefanie walking out in her scrubs.

Stefanie. Stefanie wouldn't have moved in if Katya wasn't here. Right?

"Stefanie!" Roya yelled. Stefanie, who was absorbed in her phone, startled.

"Oh," she said, looking at Roya somewhat blankly. "Hi." Her gaze moved over to Aty. "Thanks for getting the plumber in so quickly."

"No problem," Aty said, and waited until Stefanie was out the door before she turned to Roya. "Since when do you greet the tenants by their first names?"

"Since . . . ," Roya started. "I don't know. Sorry, Aty. We have to go to 3G."

She grabbed Amin's hand and raced up the stairs.

"And since when do you call me Aty?" Aty asked, her hands on her hips now. "What is going on with you?"

"I'll explain in one minute," Roya said as she thundered up the stairs.

Her heart was pounding as they stood in front of the dark burgundy door with the 3G stickers on it. Maybe it was from racing up two flights of stairs, but Roya suspected it was more than that. Things *had* changed. Surely things had changed in a good way too.

They knocked on the door. Behind them, they could hear Aty's footsteps climbing up the stairs.

"Roya," she was saying sharply. "I'm supposed to be meeting my editor for lunch and I don't have time for this. What in the world is going on?"

Her editor, Roya thought, feeling like her wildly beating heart was basking in a sudden surge of sunshine.

But it was nothing compared to her feelings when the door opened.

"Hello," Katya said, looking a little puzzled but smiling slightly, one hand on her rounded belly.

Roya's insides were a whole spray of shooting stars as she

burst into laughter and then, not being able to help herself, leaned in and threw her arms around Katya even though, she suspected, they didn't quite have that relationship. Not in this timeline, anyway. Not yet.

"Hello, Katya," she said. "Or Ms. Petrov. Or whatever I call you. It's so good to see you."

Camp Roya

OVER THE NEXT WEEK, ROYA went to camp. It was, given all she'd been through this summer, less exciting and glamorous than she'd always imagined it to be. There was a lot of bug spray, sunscreen, and schedules involved. Plus it was funny how much less appealing traveling by electric scooter seemed once you had traveled through the space–time continuum.

There was no camp in the last week before school started, so Roya divided her time between visiting Baba and getting to know Stefanie and Katya well again. Or, at least, getting them to know *her* well again.

As far as Baba was concerned, he was in the same place health–wise as he'd been every time (and in every time–line) that Roya had seen him over the past year. Frail and propped up on the couch, but still talking to Roya with his same wit and sense of humor. Roya had started broaching the subject of time travel with him—though, for now, only as a hypothetical.

"So if I had gone back to the 1940s, done something that would change this timeline, and then returned, could I have replaced a version of me who never traveled?" It was the version Roya thought of now as Camp Roya—the one who was still the super's kid but didn't spend her summers roaming around the building. She was surprised to see that the online episodes of her podcast were gone too.

Baba smiled. "I suppose so. Why all this sudden interest in time travel, huh?"

Roya shrugged. "It's cool. And fun to talk about with you."

Baba put his hand on Roya's shoulder. "I love talking to you about it too. Maybe we can find a good podcast on the subject."

Roya leaned into his thin chest, careful not to put her full body weight on him, but also happy to have him close. It seemed like there were some things that were impossible for her to change, no matter how hard she might try or wish to—barriers that may not be physical, but were there all the same. But even if it wasn't forever, the time they had now was important. And letting go of the mysteries or heartaches of the future, even if just a little, had lifted a fraction of the weight off her heart.

"Hey, Baba," she asked, hearing his pulse through his shirt.

"Hmmmm?"

"Do you remember ever seeing a piece of graffiti in Coney Island? With your name on it?" Roya already knew that Aty's books existed, so she suspected what the answer would be. But she still wouldn't mind getting the details.

"My name?" Baba asked, puzzled. "No, I don't think so."

Roya leaned away and looked back into his face. "Really? No 'Payman' and 'Khosrow and the Sea Doctor'?"

"Ah," Baba said, his eyes lighting up. "Khosrow, yes. But never my name. In fact, I randomly told your mother about that little piece of writing and she ran with it. And, of course, there was *your* name."

"My name?" Roya asked, blinking.

Baba nodded. "As soon as you were born, I remembered that 'Love, Roya' on the wall, and I knew what your name would be."

Roya looked into her baba's eyes. "Baba," she said, quickly making a decision. "What if I told you . . . that was *me* who had written that. A me who had traveled back and written it. For you."

Baba began to chuckle but then, catching the earnest look on Roya's face, stopped. "No . . . ," he started, and then stopped himself again. "Yes?" he asked Roya.

She nodded slowly, and a light came into Baba's eyes, overtaking the shadows underneath them as he gushed to his daughter in one excited breath, "Tell me *everything*."

Roya settled in deeper on the couch next to her dad with

a smile, grateful for Cornelius Lanczos and ready to share her story with the one person she knew would still believe her.

"**ARE YOU SURE MY FAMILY** is going to be interesting enough for a podcast?" Katya asked.

"One hundred percent," Roya assured her. They were in the lobby of the Queen, and Roya had her recorder with her. She apparently still owned it, along with her notebook. There were several recorded episodes about the tenants saved on her tablet too. Even if she hadn't gone so far as to post them in this timeline, there was still something about the podcast that was essentially her.

Just as the essentials of the Petrovs hadn't changed, either. When Roya found out they were getting together for an annual reunion, she'd insisted on asking if she could do a podcast episode on them. Katya had been confused but agreed. And now Roya held her recorder up to a tall, thirtysomething brunette. This was Inessa, and she had possibly the most incredible story of all of them. She was just telling them about how Annika had adopted her as a baby from an orphanage in Brighton Beach—an orphanage that just two weeks after the adoption had burned down along with all of its records.

"Did anyone get hurt?" Roya asked.

"That was the oddest thing," Inessa said. "No one was inside. It was an abandoned building."

"Even though I know I had seen other children and caretakers there just weeks before," Annika added.

Roya and Amin looked at each other. "The immutable things," Amin whispered, and Roya nodded.

"You know," said Polina, who aside from leaning on a cane didn't seem much like the hundred-year-old woman she was, "you two look awfully familiar to me. But I can't seem to place you."

Roya and Amin shared a glance before Roya said, "Maybe I just have one of those faces."

"Yeah," Amin added. "Me too."

"Hmmm," Polina said, sounding unconvinced.

"Anyway," Roya continued, changing the subject. "I don't think we have time today, but can I come by one day so you and Annika can tell me about your mother–daughter acrobat routine at the Coney Island Sideshows?"

Annika nodded, a big smile on her bright red lips. "I'd love that. It was great fun. But then again, Coney Island always has been."

"That's why they go there every year for their reunion," Stefanie said.

"*Our* reunion," Daria corrected. "You're a Petrov now."

"Our reunion," Stefanie agreed.

"And we can't wait for the newest little Petrov to join us next year," a young woman with a shock of red hair said, staring fondly at Katya's belly. She turned to Daria. "Right, Mama?"

"Oh, yes," Daria replied. Because this Daria, the one who never traveled, apparently *did* have a daughter: Tori.

"Funny you should say that, Tori," Katya said to her cousin. "Can we go ahead and book you now for babysitting?"

"Uh . . . like, without adult supervision?" Tori asked.

"Tori. *You* are the adult," Katya said.

"Says who?" Tori replied with a wry smile.

"*Anyway*," Katya said, smirking as she turned to Roya and Amin. "We should get going, but do you two want to join us? We've been spending so much time together, I feel like you're becoming a part of the family."

"Thank you," Amin said. "But it's almost lunchtime."

"We can all get Nathan's," Stefanie offered.

"Oh, Amin doesn't eat that," Roya said at the same time that Amin replied with, "No, thank you. I have my chicken nuggets waiting for me at home." Amin looked at Roya and smiled at her gratefully. But Roya felt grateful too: it felt nice to be known, sure, but it felt just as nice to know someone well.

Roya turned back to the Petrovs. "And I promised my mom we'd eat together today. But rain check?"

"Rain check," Stefanie said, nodding.

Roya and Amin said their goodbyes as Katya, Stefanie, Polina, Annika, Daria, Inessa, and Tori all bustled out the building door.

Roya watched them go. "The essentials really do seem to be in place, don't they?" Every day she was still discovering little things that were slightly different from before, and, she suspected, there were plenty of things she hadn't noticed yet. But she was okay with that. And, perhaps even more surprisingly, Amin seemed to be too.

"As far as I can tell," he said. "Everyone seems to be here. Our families. Their family. But . . ." Amin cocked his head.

"But?" Roya asked.

"I'm not sure if the non-traveling versions of us were friends this summer. My parents didn't know who you were."

Roya shrugged. "That's okay. Our friendship is immutable now." She pointed to the whistle that Amin still wore around his neck. "There's the proof." Because they had traveled with them that final time, the whistle and original lavender fortune were the only physical mementos they had of their whole adventure. The note Amin's teenaged parents had written to each other was gone from Amin's room, as was the yellow fortune the two of them had first received from Grandmother. Though neither of them had forgotten what it said.

"Proof of a great friend," Amin said as he touched the whistle now.

"Do you want to get together and record after lunch?" Roya asked.

"Okay," Amin said. "Meet you in the basement?"

"Meet you in the basement," Roya said, smiling. Her recorder might not have worked in the past, but Amin's echoic memory still did. QOOP had cohosts now and, sometimes, veered off into a fantasy adventure only the two of them could weave—together.

"Oh, wait," Roya said, her eyes widening. "I just thought of something." She ran outside the building and Amin followed her. They looked around just in time to see the Petrovs turning the corner.

"Hey! Petrovs!" Roya called out, but the large, bustling family was too deep in conversation to hear her. She ran after them, yelling, "Katya!"

The young blond woman turned around, and the rest of her family stopped too.

"We forgot to tell you to just . . . uh, stay away from any fortune-telling machines," Roya said. "If you see one."

At that, there was a flash of recognition in Polina's eyes and she gasped, but Katya, looking puzzled, asked, "Why?"

Amin and Roya looked at each other before they turned to the Petrovs and said, in unison, "Just trust us."

Acknowledgments

I OWE THE BIGGEST THANK-YOUS to two true queens: Molly Ker Hawn, my incredible, thoughtful agent and the best advocate I've ever had in my corner; and Erin Clarke, my wonderful, brilliant editor who acquired this book and knew all the right questions to ask to get Roya to where she needed to be.

I'm also immensely grateful to Katherine Harrison and Gianna Lakenauth, who took over the editing reins and helped get QOOP over the finish line. And I must make sure artist Ericka Lugo and art director Carol Ly know how much their stunning cover art makes me weepy with joy. I've always wanted a book with interior illustrations, and I'm so thrilled that it's this one and that it's Ericka's gorgeous work that graces it. Also huge thank-yous to everyone who worked on this book at Knopf, including Natalia Dextre, Jake Eldred, Melinda Ackell, Alison Kolani, Christine Ma, and Lisa Leventer.

I wrote a lot of this book while on two writing retreats at the incredible Highlights campus and am so grateful to the authors who were on those retreats with me, giving me so much encouragement while also walking me through (with diagrams!) the concept of time loops: Lauren Magaziner, Tiffany Schmidt, Miranda Kenneally, Jessica Spotswood, Eric Smith, and Rebecca Behrens.

I also have to thank: Margaret Solow, for casually dropping the title of this book in a conversation years ago; my neighborhood and the lovely neighbors in it who make it such an incredible place to live; Dr. Lauren Sosenko for helping me unlock so much about why I was writing this book; my family, particularly my sister Golnaz for being the built-in best friend I always needed; my father-in-law, Michael, who talked through some of the time-travel logistics with me; and my husband, Graig, for always letting me talk my plotting problems at him until I figure them out. And, most of all, thank you to my kids, the real Bennett and Jonah, who inspired every aspect of this story. Everything I ever wanted to say to you is in here, with all my love, from your mama.